Edward Armstrong, Thomas Budd

**Good Order Established in Pennsylvania and New-Jersey**

in America, being a true account of the country - with its produce and commodities

there made in the year 1685

Edward Armstrong, Thomas Budd

**Good Order Established in Pennsylvania and New-Jersey**
*in America, being a true account of the country - with its produce and commodities there made in the year 1685*

ISBN/EAN: 9783337230937

Printed in Europe, USA, Canada, Australia, Japan

Cover: Foto ©Andreas Hilbeck / pixelio.de

More available books at **www.hansebooks.com**

# GOWANS'

# BIBLIOTHECA AMERICANA.

# 4

"I look into the times of old, but they seem dim, like reflecting moonbeams, on a distant, placid lake."............................*Ossian.*

"Civil History, it is of three kinds; not unfitly to be compared with three kinds of pictures or images we see; some are unfinished, some are perfect, and some are defaced. So of histories we may find three kinds, Memorials, Perfect Histories, and Antiquities; for Memorials are history unfinished, or the first or rough draughts of history; and Antiquities are history defaced, or some remnants of history which have casually escaped the shipwreck of time. Histories make men wise, poets witty; the mathematics, subtile; natural philosophy, deep, moral, grave; logic and rhetoric, able to contend; "*Abeunt studia in mores.*"............................*Lord Bacon.*

NEW YORK:

WILLIAM GOWANS.

1865.

# GOOD ORDER

ESTABLISHED IN

# PENNSYLVANIA AND NEW-JERSEY

IN

# AMERICA,

BEING A TRUE ACCOUNT OF THE COUNTRY; WITH ITS PRODUCE AND
COMMODITIES THERE MADE IN THE YEAR 1685.

## BY THOMAS BUDD.

A NEW EDITION WITH AN INTRODUCTION AND COPIOUS HISTORICAL NOTES.

## BY EDWARD ARMSTRONG,

MEMBER OF THE HISTORICAL SOCIETY OF PENNSYLVANIA, &C.,

*Who loves fair nature, fails not here to find*
*Her charms in all variety combined ;*
*Her magic hand profuse has here bestowed*
*Hill, valley, mountain, glen, and foaming flood,*
*Innum'rous islets crowned with shrubs and flowers,*
*Moisten'd with rainbow spray, and sparkling showers,*
*Sweetly bestrew each river's craggy bed,*
*While frowning rocks above, their sorrow spread ;*
*Meadows and groves enrobed in living green,*
*Adorn their banks and deck the beauteous scene.*—DRYDEN.

" Agriculture is so universally understood among them, that neither man nor
woman is ignorant of it. They are instructed in it from their childhood, partly
at school and partly by practice, being frequently led into the fields near the town,
where they not only see others at work, but become exercised in it themselves.
Beside agriculture, so common to them, every man hath some peculiar trade, as
the manufacture of wool or flax, masonry, smith's or carpenter's work. They
wear one sort of clothes, without any other distinction than what is necessary
for different sexes, and the married and unmarried. The fashion never changes,
is easy and agreeable, suited to the climate, and for summer as well as winter.
SIR THOMAS MORE.

NEW YORK:

WILLIAM GOWANS.

1865.

May 17th, 1866
115 Nassau St,

Dear Sir,

I beg to take the liberty of making the following enquiry of you, namely, have you in your possession a copy of an old book relating to America entitled "Alsop's Maryland", and if so would you do me the favor of alowing me to take a copy of it in manuscript?

In the event of dooing so, I intend to make it No 5 of the series of early tracts on the settlement of the British Colonies in America four of which I have already published.

I beg your acceptance of a copy of No 4 of that publication Budel's Account of Pennsylvania 1685. Edited

by Edward Armstrong Esq. which
the bearer will hand to you,
the other three I presume you
already have.

I am your most
Obedient servent

William Gowan

Mr. George Bancroft —
17 West 21st St —

# ADVERTISEMENT.

The subscriber announces to the public, that he intends publishing a series of works, relating to the history, literature, biography, antiquities and curiosities of the Continent of America. To be entitled

## GOWANS' BIBLIOTHECA AMERICANA.

The books to form this collection, will chiefly consist of reprints from old and scarce works, difficult to be produced in this country, and often also of very rare occurrence in Europe; occasionally an original work will be introduced into the series, designed to throw light upon some obscure point of American history, or to elucidate the biography of some of the distinguished men of our land. Faithful reprints of every work published will be given to the public; nothing will be added, except in the way of notes, or introduction, which will be presented entirely distinct from the body of the work. They will be brought out in the best style, both as to the type, press work and paper, and in such a manner as to make them well worthy a place in any gentleman's library.

A part will appear about once every six months, or oftener, if the public taste demand it; each part forming an entire work, either an original production, or a reprint of some valuable, and at the same time scarce tract. From eight or twelve parts will form a handsome octavo volume, which the publisher is well assured, will be esteemed entitled to a high rank in every collection of American history and literature.

Should reasonable encouragement be given, the whole collection may in the course of no long period of time become not less voluminous, and quite as valuable to the student in American history, as the celebrated Harleian Miscellany is now to the student and lover of British historical antiquities.

W. GOWANS, *Publisher.*

# INTRODUCTION.

*Thomas Budd*[1] the author of this book, was the son of the Rev. Thomas Budd, of the parish of Martock,[2] Somersetshire, England. The latter was "an established preacher of the national church, and having been convinced of the truth as professed by the Quakers, separated himself from that church, renounced his benefice, and became a minister of the gospel, without money and without price.[3]" He did not flinch from what he conceived to be the line of duty, and having permitted a meeting for religious worship to be held at his house, which the rabble broke in upon and dispersed, was arrested as a disturber of the peace, and although discharged from custody the end was not yet.[4] Persecution for opinion sake raged throughout England; the most cruel opposition followed any attempt to exercise religious

[1] Fac-simile autograph of the author.

[2] MARTOCK, SOMERSETSHIRE, a parish and market town in the hundred of Martock on the river Parret, 166 miles from London. * * The town consists chiefly of one long street with a market house near the centre. The living *All Saints*, a discharged vicarage, with the curacy of Lond in the Archdeanry of Wells and Diocese of Bath and Wells at present has a value of £194. Parish contains 6,930 acres; established population in 1819, 3,479. See 3d vol. Clarke's *British Gaz.*, Lond., 1852.

[3] Besse's *Sufferings of the Quakers*, I, 580, in note.

[4] See note at end of introduction.

2

liberty. Budd was a marked man. In 1661 he was required to take the " oath of obedience" prescribed by the statute 1st James I, passed "for the better discovering of papist recusants."

Although willing to affirm, and entirely loyal, he could not take an oath and comply with the requirements of an oppressive statute perverted to an oppressive purpose. He was arrested, indicted, found guilty, and receiving sentence of præmunire, lingered out his few remaining years in the jail at Ilchester, where he died on the 22d of June, 1670, firm in his faith.[1]

The father's dying wish was answered. Thomas Budd attached himself to the society of Friends, and leaving England arrived at Burlington, New Jersey, in the year 1678, an ardent upholder of the rights of conscience, thoroughly imbued with the spirit of liberty, and ready to lend his influence to their fundamental establishment "for all people" within the province.

John Cripps, in a letter dated at that place 19th 4 m., 1678, and written to a relation in England, refers to Budd as having had " far more experience" of West Jersey than some other individual, whose name he does not give, " could have had in the short time he was among us." The writer further states that Budd also had written " and endeavored to satisfy, as near as he could, of the truth of things."[2]

[1] " A faithful man, having been a prisoner at Ilchester about 8 years and 4 months under sentence of præmunire, departed this life in much peace, declaring some hours before his death that he had renewed his engagements and covenants with God, and was therein well satisfied, and expressed a firm hope and belief, that God would support him as in life, so in death, with the right hand of his righteousness. He also rejoiced and praised God that his children did walk in the way of the Lord."—*Besse*, I, 609.

[2] Smith's *New Jersey*, 100, 108.

From this we conclude that Budd came in the beginning of 1678.[1] During his residence in West Jersey he held several important offices and was a leading man in the province.

In the year 1681, he was, by act of Assembly, appointed with Thomas Gardiner one of the receivers general to collect £200 for the purpose of defraying the debts of the province, and in the same year was chosen one of the commissioners for "settling and regulation of lands," a member of the governor's council and one of the regulators of weights and measures.[2]

In 1682 and '83, he was elected to the Assembly and rechosen land commissioner and councillor, and in the

[1] The following is a list of all the vessels which arrived in the Delaware from Great Britain between the years 1675 and 1679. It is probably not complete, although there is no available source within our knowledge to make it more so. After 1679 the arrivals were much more numerous.

The "Griffith," from London, arrived in 1675 with Fenwicke and his company, and landed at the spot called by him Salem. Smith, p. 79, says this was the first English ship that came to West Jersey, and Proud states (I, 137), that "it was near two years before another followed," which was the "Kent," Gregory Marlow, master, and which arrived from London at New Castle, 16, 6m., August, 1677.—Smith, 93. "Phenix," Matthew Shearer, master, arrived 6th m., 1677.—From a copy in possession of editor of a MS. Registry of Arrivals. "Flie Boat Martha," of Burlington, Yorkshire, sailed from Hull in Aug., 1677.—Smith, 102. A copy of MS. Registry of Arrivals says the Martha, Thomas Wildtuys, master, arrived in 7th m., 1677. "Willing Mind," John Newcomb, master, from London, arrived Nov., 1677.—Smith, 102. MS. Registry of Arrivals says 28th 7th m., 1677. "Shield," of Hull, Daniel Towes, master, arrived 10th month (O. S.), 1678. —Smith, 108. "Elizabeth and Sarah," Richard Ffriend, master, arrived 29th 3 m., 1679.—MS. Registry. "Elizabeth and Mary," of Weymouth, arrived 4th 4th m., 1679.—MS. Registry. "Jacob and Mary," Richard Moore, master, arrived 12th 7th m., 1679.—MS. Registry.

[2] Smith, 130, 152; see also Leaming and Spicer's Laws.

latter year with Thomas Gardiner again commissioned one of the treasurers of the province.[1]

Budd and Francis Collins, in 1683, were each to have 1,000 acres, "parts of lands to be purchased of the Indians above the falls," the present site of Trenton, N. J., in consideration and discharge for building a market and court house, at Burlington.[2]

And in the same year Budd was appointed by the Assembly to draw up a letter to Edward Byllinge, and also an instrument containing the state of the case of the proprietors with Edward Byllinge.[3]

Such was the satisfaction he gave in the handling of this business that it led to further employment in it.

In 1684 the Assembly resolved "that the matter relating to the demand and consideration of the right of the corporation and freeholders to the government, against Edward Byllinge's pretence to the same, be proceeded in, and a demand to Edward Byllinge for his confirmation of what he hath sold be first made" and Budd, with Thomas Jennings, were appointed to negotiate the affair in England.

The poverty of the province was such that it was unable to provide funds to defray the expenses and salaries of its commissioners, and Jennings and Budd with Thomas Oliver became bound for 100 pounds sterling in the public account for the charges of the commission, and received fifteen hundred acres above the falls as their security, the title to be made when the land was purchased of the Indians.[4]

In 1684 Budd sailed upon his mission, and it was during his stay in England that *Good Order* was published, and

[1] Leaming and Spicer's Laws, 442, 445, 458.   [2] Idem., 467.   [3] Idem., 482.
[4] Idem, 485, 487.

which appears to have been given to the printer on the 25th of October, 1685.

In the latter end of the year he returned to West Jersey, and was with his brother, James Budd, chosen a member of the Assembly, and became one of the chief promoters in the erection of the new Meeting House at Burlington.[1]

This, so far as the records inform, was his last appearance in public life in that province, and it is likely he shortly afterwards removed to Philadelphia, for on the 17th 9th m., 1685, he petitioned the provincial council of the province of Pennsylvania for a special court to end a difference between Philip Th: Lehman and himself.[2] He probably at this time began to give his attention to mercantile pursuits.

We meet no further reference to him until the 7th of 12th mo., 1688-9, when we find his application to the provincial council of Pennsylvania conjointly with others representing their "design in setting up a bank for money, and requesting incouragement from the governor's council for their proceeding therein." Blackwell, Penn's deputy governor, replied "that some things of this nature had been proposed and dedicated to the proprietor by *himself* some months since," that he hoped shortly to hear from Penn and *encouragingly* suggested that he knew "no reason why they might not give their personall bills to such as would take them as money, to pass as Merchants usually did bills of exchange, but that it might be suspected that such as usually clipp'd or coyned money would be apt to counterfeit their bills unless more than ordinary care were taken to prevent it which might be their ruine, as well as ye peoples that should deal with

---

[1] Idem., 602.  [2] Provincial Minutes of Pa., 163.

them.''[1]  Although Budd's name does not head the petition we little doubt that he was the originator of the movement, as he had already, in his tract. urged the establishment of a bank, and that the mind of Blackwell had been directed to project by the arguments which Budd had already put into print.  The information volunteered by the governor was not new to the petitioners, and if we hear no more about the establishment of a bank the seed sown by Budd did not lie dormant, and the scheme whose utility our author had so well recommended in his publication. eventually took shape in the erection of a Loan Office, whereby all the benefits Budd had predicted happily resulted.

The public spirit manifested by Budd was exhibited in an enterprise, the first of the kind attempted in Philadelphia.  Having become. about the year 1689 or 1690, the owner of property on the west side of Front street, adjoining the Draw Bridge, or dock, at the Blue Anchor Tavern on the south, and extending along Front street towards Walnut street. he erected a row of houses which were known as Budd's Row or Budd's Buildings.  Two of the original houses were standing in the beginning of this century.

In 1689 he again went to England and returned to Philadelphia in the following year.

In 1691 the unhappy schism occurred in the society of Friends by the desertion of George Keith.  Some of the principal persons who adhered to Keith, and were men of rank, character and reputation in these provinces, and divers of them great preachers, and much followed, were Thomas Budd, &c.[2]

As in all convulsions, civil or religious, so in this, the

---

[1] Provincial Min. of Penn., I, 236.  [2] I. Proud, 369, in note.

father was often found arrayed against the son, and brother against brother, and the melancholy result of the breach was visible for many years. Keith was properly disowned by the society in 1692, and doubtless also Budd, although we discover no evidence of that fact upon record. The schism produced, as is usual on such occasions, an abundance of published controversy.

Samuel Jennings had rendered himself obnoxious to Keith, and the latter in a publication entitled *Plea of the Innocents*, reflected upon Jennings' and the magistracy. The result was a presentation by the grand jury of Philadelphia, of Keith and Budd as the authors of the attack, an eventual trial, and a sentence of £5 against each, which was however never exacted.[1] Budd did not desert Keith but fully identified himself with his cause, and finally went to England with him in 1694 to defend him before the yearly meeting.

From this year, 1694, to the period of his death, or rather of the date of the probate of his will at Philadelphia, that is in March, 1698, we find little about Budd. We have no information as to his age or personal appearance. His will indicates the possession of no real estate, save that which he devised to his son Thomas, and in which his son lived, "being the corner house nearest the dock." To his two daughters he gives £100 each, and his will contains no residuary clause.

The inventory of his personal effects amounts to but 457 pounds, although from the records and the account filed by his executor, who was his eldest son, and his mercantile partner, he owned other real estate than that mentioned in his will. By his wife Susanna, who survived him, and was a prominent Friend and who adhered

[1] Idem., 373.

to the society, he appears to have had four children ; John, the eldest son, to whom we have referred, and of whom more presently ; Thomas, who died at Philadelphia in 1699, leaving issue, Mary and George, whose descendants we are unable to trace, and daughters Mary, born at Burlington, 2d 7th mo., 1679, who married William Allen and was an ancestress of Chief Justice Allen, of the supreme court of the province of Pennsylvania, and Rose, also born at Burlington, 13th 1st month, 1680, but of whom we know nothing more.

John, the eldest son, and who it seems was at one time sheriff of Philadelphia county, having left and been probably disowned by the society, became a Presbyterian and active in the religious concerns of the First Presbyterian Church of Philadelphia, then under the charge of the Rev. Jedediah Andrews. He afterwards removed to the township of *New Hanover*, then in Hunterdon, now in the eastern part of Morris county, New Jersey, adhering to his adopted faith and attaching himself to the church at Hanover, or Whippany as it was sometimes called.[1] He held the position for many years of agent to the Proprietaries. In his will recorded in the office of secretary of state at Trenton, dated Sept. 6, 1749, and proved 16 May, 1754, in which latter year we presume he died, he states he was "very aged." His wife Sarah survived him and he had several children although we can give the name of but one, *Berne*, who left sons John C., and David, and a daughter Sarah. John C., just named, also left sons, Berne W., a physician, and Vincent, both dead, and John S., who still lives near Chatham, N. J., and eight daughters. David, already mentioned, had issue, William T., Israel W., and one daughter. John Budd, the son of the author,

---

[1] Webster's *Hist. of the Presb. Church*, 315, 415, 482.

was the owner of considerable real estate in Philadelphia, and its vicinity, and of some 20,000 acres of land in New Jersey. We are informed, however, that these large possessions were of little avail to his descendants, from the fact that his widow, having married his former agent, joined with the latter in conveying land; and the titles thus attempted to be made were for so long a time allowed to remain unimpeached that the statute of limitations barred the prosecution of any claim.

Our author had several brothers, *James*, of whom we have spoken and who was drowned at Burlington; *John*, who died at Philadelphia in 1704 without issue, and *William* Budd, who died in 1723 at his farm in Northampton Township, Burlington County, about four miles west of Mount Holly, and who by his will left a benefaction to the Episcopal Church of St. Mary's at Burlington, of which he appears to have been a steadfast member, and where he is buried, and also land in Northampton Township[1], on which to build a Church. His descendants are very numerous in Pennsylvania, and in southern New Jersey, and we believe that with the exception of those of the name who trace their origin to Thomas Budd, and who are comparatively few, all the rest in the regions referred to are descended from the first William. Rachel Budd, a grand-daughter of the latter, married Wm. Bradford, whose ancestor was the famous printer of that name, and became the mother of Wm. Bradford, born 14 Sept., 1753, and who was appointed in 1794, by Washington, Attorney General of the United States. Ann, a daughter of the first William Budd, married James Bingham, whose descendant

---

[1] "I give unto the Episcopal Church of England 100 acres of land, reserved out of my son's, for a Church to be built thereon, and a school to be kept ; the said Church to be built thereon within ten years after my decease."
—Will of *William Budd, of Northampton,* made 1708.—*Records at Trenton.*

3

Ann, the daughter of William Bingham, intermarried with Alexander Baring, whose son, Wm. Bingham Baring, became Lord Ashburton.

A work quaintly entitled: "England's Improvement by Sea and Land. To outdo the *Dutch* without fighting. To pay debts without money. To set at work all the poor of England with the growth of our own Lands. To prevent unnecessary suits in Law. With the benefit of a voluntary Register, &c., by Andrew Yarranton,[1] Gent., London, 1677," 8vo, pp. 195, is copiously quoted by Budd, and doubtless suggested to him the composition of this tract.

It does not, however, in the least diminish Budd's merits as an author that he should have had a model and have

[1] Yarranton, at the end of his book gives the following curious account of himself and his various employments. "I was an Apprentice to a Linnen Draper when this King was born (Charles II), and continued at the Trade some years. But the shop being too narrow and short for my large mind, I took leave of my Master, but said nothing. Then I lived a country life for some years, and in the late Wars I was a soldier, and sometimes had the honor and misfortune to lodge and dislodge an Army: In the year one thousand six hundred and fifty-two, I entered upon Iron works, and pli'd them several years, and in these times I made it my business to survey the three great rivers of England, and some small ones ; and made two navigable and a third almost completed.  *  *  *  If any gentleman, or others please to put pen to paper in opposition to what is here asserted I shall give him a civil return, bound up with the second part, where these seven heads shall be Treated on." His 6th head contains the following announcement.

"6thly. How to employ six thousand young lawyers, and three thousand Priests, for the good of the Public and mankind, who now have neither practice nor cure of souls."

Yarranton published besides his "England's Improvement," another work entitled "Yarranton's Improvement by Clover."

Some account may be found of him in "Dove's Elements of Political Science, pp. 402-470, Lond., 8vo, 1854," which account has also been published separately in 12mo, and the best biographical sketch is in Smile's Industrial Biography, pp. 60-76, Lond., 8vo, 1863.

freely used it, for no one can read this production without being struck with the forecast and originality of many of his views, and above all, with the public spirit which inspired the publication of a work whose sole aim seems to have been, to set forth to his countrymen the advantages presented in the choice of a new home in the wilderness of Pennsylvania and New Jersey.

The publisher has done good service to the historical student in selecting it as one of his valuable series of books relating to American history.

We beg to express our acknowledgments to the Rev. John M. Thomson, of Hanover, N. J.; Miss Sarah B. Comly, of Biberry Philad.; Messrs. Nathan Kite, and John William Wallace, of Philadelphia, for information concerning Thomas and William Budd; to Mr. J. D. Hall (in office of the Secretary of State, Trenton), for facilities in examining records; to Dr. E. B. O'Callaghan, of Albany, and Mr. William A. Whitehead, of Newark, for valuable references, and to Messrs. Wm. J. Allinson and C. Baquet, of Burlington, N. J.

### NOTE.

The following is the account of Budd's examination, and to which reference has been made on the first page of the introduction. It is a picture of the times, and proves how straightforwardness and honest shrewdness sometimes baffle those who seek to entrap.

The history of the persecution of the Quakers is full of examples as striking as this selected, in which the parties questioned were driven by the replies received to conclusions as undesirable as they were unexpected —into dilemmas from which there was no escape even by equivocation.

"On the 7th of the month called April, this year (1657) was a meeting at the house of Thomas Budd, in the parish of Martock, to which five Priests came, attended by a rabble furnished with staves, cudgels, pitch-forks and such like rustic arms. They rushed into the meeting with so much confusion and noise that the preacher could not be heard. Their coming indeed made it a riotous assembly, which the moment before was a congregation of grave and serious Christians of sober and virtuous conver-sation, and some of them of considerable estates. However, the Priest who brought the mob and caused the riot, complained to the magistrates that the meeting held at Thomas Budd's was a riotous assembly, to the destruction of the public peace. Whereupon one Captain Raymond, with his soldiers, was ordered to disperse the next meeting that shou'd be held there. Accordingly he came thither on the 23d of the same month, when Thomas Salthouse was preaching and took him, together with Thomas Budd, into custody, and conducted them next day to Robert Hunt, Justice of the Peace, they were by him and others examined.

*Justices.* What is your name?

*T. S.* Thomas Salthouse.

*Justices.* Do you acknowledge subjection to the present government of this Nation?

*T. S.* I own the higher power, and the wholesome laws of this land, which are grounded upon the law of equity, by which I stand to be judged, and am now brought before you in submission to the present gov-ernment by Captain Raymond's order. I expect the privilege of a free born Englishman, to wit: Liberty of conscience, to wait upon and worship God in spirit, according as is exprest in the Instrument of government.

*Justices.* We require you to be uncovered before the Magistrate.

*T. S.* I am sensible that I am in the presence of the Lord God of Heaven and Earth, and I know of no offence in standing before Him with my hat on; and if it be no offence to Him, who is the Lord and Master, I hope its none to moderate men, though magistrates, that are but his ser-vants.

\*    \*    \*    \*    \*    \*    \*    \*    \*    \*    \*    \*    \*

*Justices.* How are you maintained? How do you live?

*T. S.* I want for nothing; I have food and raiment, and am therewith content.

*Justices.* An highwayman would say so much for himself.

317

*T. S.* Do you look upon me to be such an one? To whom have I been burdensome? or where is mine accuser that hath any thing to lay to my charge?

*Justices.* Here is Captain Raymond doth accuse you.

*T. S.* It's well he is present. His words cannot be wrested. Captain Raymond! What hast thou to lay to my charge, or accuse me of?

*Capt. Raymond.* You slighted me, and gave me no good account of your business, or whence you came, or where you lived.

*T. S.* That was not a fit time to examine me, the company being in confusion and disorder and several speaking to me who had no authority. Though I denied not to answer them, nor do I now deny either my name, birth, or outward habitation. I have a father and mother living, who have a good estate in the outward, from whom I have been, and may expect to be, supplied, when I have need of anything in the outward.

*Justices.* There is a scripture that you little mind: He that will not work, neither let him eat.

*T. S.* I own that scripture, and must answer you with another: Cursed is he that doth the work of the Lord negligently.

### BUDD'S EXAMINATION.

\* \* \* \* \* \* \* \* \* \* \* \*

*Justice Hunt.* Do you know what calling he is of? (Referring to Salthouse).

*T. B.* I know not of what calling he hath been formerly, but I believe he is called to preach the gospel.

*Justice Hunt.* What ground have you to believe that he is called to the ministry?

*T. B.* Because the word preached by him has reached my heart.

*Priest Walker.* Can you own that man to be a true minister, that will not acknowledge the scriptures to be the word of God? What say you Mr. Budd. Are the scriptures the word of God, yea, or no?

*T. B.* Christ is the word; and the scriptures a true declaration of him.

*Priest.* But do you own the scriptures, both of the old and new testament, to be truth?

*T B.* Yea, I do.

*Priest.* Gentlemen, I shall desire you to give me leave to ask Mr. Budd some further questions.

*T. B.* Thou art no Justice of the Peace, therefore I am not bound to answer thee.

*Priest.* But seeing the gentlemen have given me liberty, let me ask you did you ever take tithes when you were a minister?

*T. B.* I have never sued any man for tithes, while I acted as a minister in the national way; and if any are free to give their tithes to the minister I have nothing against it; but for ministers to enforce the payment of tithes from the people by lawsuits, I know no law in scripture that will warrant such a practice.

*Justice Hunt.* If men were free to pay these dues, the minister would have no need to sue them.

*T. B.* Possibly they may not profit by their ministry and therefore they are not free to pay them.

*Justice Hunt.* Though they are evil ministers, yet the people are not to withold their dues from them; for Judas had a maintenance as well as the rest of the Apostles.

*T. B.* If any are free to maintain a Judas, they may use their liberty. I desire to ask one question more of Mr. Budd: Do you own the resurrection of the just and unjust?

*T. B.* Yea, I do.

\* \* \* \* \* \* \* \* \* \* \* \* \*

*Justice Cary.* Mr. Budd, your friends are much grieved that you have been a man so much given to change.

*T. B.* I wish all my friends would turn all their grief into grief for their own sins. And not only I, but Paul himself doth witness a change, saying of himself, that he was a persecutor, a blasphemer and injurious, but God shewed mercy.

*Justice Hunt.* Did not you preach Christ formerly, when you were a minister?

*T. B.* Yea, I did preach Christ in a national manner, but now I witness him in life and power.

*Justice Hunt.* Do you own magistrates and government?

*T. B.* Yea, I do.

*Justice Hunt.* Is not honor due to magistrates?

*T. B.* Yea, to such magistrates as are a terror to evil doers.

*Priest.* But there is honor due to evil magistrates.

*T. B.* What, as being evil?

*Priest.* Yea.

*T. B.* *Wilt thou set it down in writing under thy hand?*

*Justice Hunt.* Nay, it is not due to them as evil but as magistrates.

*T. B.* This I own: That there is honor due to the power, for there is no power but of God.

*Justice Hunt.* Do you then distinguish between the person and the power?

*T. B.* Yea.

*Justice Hunt.* So then it seems there is honor due to the power, but none to the person: How then is this honor expressed?

*T. B.* Not by flattering titles and compliments, but by love, service, duty and obedience." — Besse's *Sufferings of the Quakers*, 1, 578.

This examination shows with what a noble spirit of undaunted innocence and intrepidity these men maintained their religious right of assembling together for the worship of God, for which they stood ready to sacrifice their liberty, and even life itself. Notwithstanding this convincing proof, both of the meekness and magnanimity by which true Christian sufferers in the cause of a good conscience are supported, the issue was that the justices sent Thomas Salthouse to prison.

*Good Order Eftablifhed*

IN

Pennfilvania & New-Jerfey

IN

# AMERICA,

Being a true Account of the Country;
With its Produce and Commodities there made.

And the great Improvements that may be made by
means of 𝕻𝖚𝖇𝖑𝖎𝖈𝖐 𝕾𝖙𝖔𝖗𝖊=𝖍𝖔𝖚𝖋𝖊𝖘 for 𝕳𝖊𝖒𝖕,
𝕱𝖑𝖆𝖝 and 𝕷𝖎𝖓𝖓𝖊𝖓=𝕮𝖑𝖔𝖙𝖍; alfo, the Advantages
of a 𝕻𝖚𝖇𝖑𝖎𝖈𝖐=𝕾𝖈𝖍𝖔𝖔𝖑, the Profits of a 𝕻𝖚𝖇𝖑𝖎𝖈𝖐=
𝕭𝖆𝖓𝖐, and the Probability of its arifing, if thofe
directions here laid down are followed. With
the advantages of publick 𝕲𝖗𝖆𝖓𝖆𝖗𝖎𝖊𝖘.
Likewife, feveral other things needful to be underftood by thofe that are or do intend to be concerned in planting in the faid Countries.
All which is laid down very plain, in this fmall
Treatife ; it being eafie to be underftood by any
ordinary Capacity. To which the *Reader* is
referred for his further fatisfaction.

By *Thomas Budd.*

Printed in the Year 1685.

Those that have generous Spirits, whose desires and
Endeavours are to bring the Creation into
Order, do I dedicate This, the first
Fruits of my Endeavours.

I *Taking into consideration the distressed Condition
that many thousand Families lie under in my
Native Country, by reason of the deadness of Trade, and
want of work, and believing that many that have great
store of Money that lies by them unimploy'd, would be
willing and ready to assist and encourage those poor distressed People, by supplying them with Monies, in order
to bring them out of that Slavery and Poverty they groan
under, if they might do it with safety to themselves.
These Considerations put me on writing this small Treatise, wherein I hope the Reader will have full Satisfaction,
that the Rich may help to relieve the Poor, and yet reap
great Profit and Advantage to themselves by their so doing,
which if it so happen that Rich and Poor are benefitted
by following the Advice here given, then will be answered
to the hearty Desires of.* (See note No. 1).

Your True and Well-wishing Friend
THOMAS BVDD.

It is to be noted, that the Government [of these
Countries is so settled by Consessions, and such care
taken by the establishment of certain fundamental
Laws, by which every Man's Liberty and Property,
both as Men and Christians, are preserved; so that
non shall be hurt in his Person, Estate or Liberty for
his Religious Perswasion or Practice in Worship towards God. (See note No. 2).

323

PENNSYLVANIA and *New-Jersey* in *America* lieth about forty and forty two Degrees of North Latitude, and is severed the one from the other by the River of *Delaware* on the West, and separated from *New York* Collony by *Sandy-hoock-Bay*, and part of *Hudsons* River on the East. The dayes in the Winter are about two hours longer. and in the Summer two hours shorter than in *England*, the Summer somewhat hotter, which causeth the Fruits and Corn somewhat to ripen faster than in *England*, and the Harvest for *Wheat*, *Rye* and *Barley*, being about the latter end of *June*. In the Winter season it is cold and freezing Weather, and sometimes Snow, but commonly very clear and Sun-shine, which soon dissolves it. (See note No. 3).

The Country is well Watered, the River of *Delaware* being navigable for Ships of great burthen to *Burlington* (see note No. 4), which from the *Capes*, or entrance, is accounted an hundred and forty Miles; and for Sloops to the Falls, which is about ten miles farther.

The Bay of *Sandy-Hoock* (see note No. 5). on *East-Jersey* is a safe and excellent Harbour for any Fleet of Ships, which can lie there in all Weathers. and go in

and out to Sea in Winter, as well as Summer, and
Ships of great Burthen can lie close to the Town of
*New-Perth.* (see note No. 6) which renders it a good
Scituation for Navigation, from whence in six Hours
time at most, Ships can go out into the Sea; and
close by the Town of *Perth* runs up *Rariton* River.
From the Falls of *Delaware* River the *Indians* go in
Cannows up the said River, to an *Indian* Town called
*Minisincks*, which is accounted from the Falls about
eighty miles; but this they perform by great Labour
in setting up against the Stream ; but they can come
down with ease and speed; the River from the Falls
runs from the North and North-West about twenty
miles, as I my self observed in my Travel so far by
the River, but by the *Indians* Information, it cometh
about more Easterly farther up. I have been informed, that about *Minisincks* (see note No. 7), by the
Rivar-side, both in *New-Jersey* and *Pennsylvania* is
great quantities of exceeding rich open Land, which
is occasioned by washing down of the Leaves and Soil
in great Rains from the Mountains, which Land is
exceeding good, for the raising of *Hemp* and *Flax*,
*Wheat*, or any other sorts of Corn. Fruits, Roots &c.
Where in time may be conveniently settled a Manufacture for the making of *Linnen Cloth*, *Cordage*,
*Twine, Sacking, Fishing-Nets*, and all other commodities commonly made of Hemp or Flax : And after
great Rains, we may bring down great quantities of
Goods in flat-bottom-Boats, built for that purpose,

which will then come down, by reason of the Land-floods with speed.

And into this River, betwixt the Capes and the Falls, run many navigable Rivers and Cricks, some of them fifteen or twenty Miles, and others less, which Rivers and Cricks are made by the plenty of Springs and Brooks, that run out of the Country, many of which Brooks are so considerable, as to be fit to drive Mills. And above the falls, in travelling of twenty Miles by the Rivers side, I went over twenty runnings of water, five or six of them being fit to build Mills on.

The Country for the most part is pretty leavel, until we come about ten Miles above the Falls, where it is Mountanious for many Miles, but interlaced with fertile Valleys. The Bay and River of *Delaware*, and the Rivers and Cricks that runs into it, are plentifully stored with various sorts of good *Fish* and *Water-Fowl* as *Swans*, *Geese*, *Ducks*, *Wigeons*, &c. And a considerable *Whale*-Fishery (see note No. 8), may be carried on in the Bay of *Delaware*, and on the Sea-Coasts of *New-Jersey*, there being *Whale*-Fisheries already begun, plenty of *Whales* being by experience found there, and the Winter-time being the time for the catching them, they will not thereby be hindred of raising there Summer-Crops; and the Oyl and Bone being good commodities to be sent for *England*, there also being in the Bay of *Delaware* and *Sandy-Hook*, *Drums*, *Sheeps-Heads*, *Bass*, and other sorts of large

Fish, which may be fit to salt up in Casks to keep for use, and Transportation also.  There are great plenty of *Oysters*, which may be pickled and put up in small Casks for use.  Likewise, in *Delaware* River are great plenty of *Sturgion*, which doubtless might be a good Trade, if mannaged by such Persons as are skilful in the boyling and pickling of them, so as to preserve them good to *Barbadoes*, and other adjacent Islands. There are also in the Spring great quantities of a sort of Fish like *Herrings:* with plenty of the Fish called *Shads*, but not like the *Shads* in *England*, but of another kind, being a much better sort of Fish ; the Inhabitants usually catch quantities, which they salt up, and pack them in Barrels for Winter's Provision.

The Lands from the Capes, to about six Miles above *New-Castle* (which is by estimation ninety Miles) is for the most part very rich, there being very many navigable Cricks on both sides of the River, and on the River and Cricks are great quantities of rich fat Marsh Land, which causeth those parts, to some fresh People, to be somewhat unhealthful in the latter part of the Summer, at which time some of them have *Agues :* Also in and near these Marshes, are small Flies, called *Musketoes*, which are troublesome to such People as are not used to them ; but were those Marshes banked, and drained, and then plowed and sowed, some Years with Corn, and then with *English* Hay-seed, I do suppose it would be healthful, and very little troubled with *Musketoes;* and if Cattle did commonly feed on this Ground, and tread it as in *England*, I suppose it would not be inferior to the rich Meadows on the River of *Thames ;* and were quantities of this Land laid dry, and brought into Tillage, I suppose it would bear great Crops of *Wheat, Pease* and *Barley, Hemp,* and *Flax,* and it would be very fit for *Hop-Gardens,* and for *English* Grass, which might serve for rich Pastures or Meadow. Also these Marshes are fit for *Rape,* and were *Rape-*Mills built, and the design managed, so as it would be if it were in *England* or *Holland,* a great Trade might be carried on, and many hundred Tuns of *Rape-*Oyl might be made yearly, and sent to *England,* to the Planters inrichment ; and not only so, but would be for Merchants advantage, they thereby having Goods to freight their Ships, which would tend to the benefit of the Inhabitants in general.

And if those Trades and Designs are carried on to effect, as are mentioned in this Treatise, there would naturally follow Trade and Imployment for *Ship-wrights, Boat-wrights, Coopers, Carpenters, Smiths, Ropers, Mariners, Weavers, Butchers. Bakers, Brewers ;* and many other sorts of Trades would have full Imployment.

From six Miles above *New-Castle* to the Falls of *Delaware* (which is about sixty Miles) and so to the Head of the said River, the *Water* is clear, fresh, and fit for Brewing, or any other use.

The *Air* clear and good, it being supposed to be as healthful as any part of *England.*

The *Land* is in Veins, some good, and some bad,

but the greatest part will bear good Corn, as *Wheat*, *Rye*, *Barley*, *Oats*, *Indian Corn*, *Buck-Wheat*, *Pease* and *Indian Beans*, *&c.*

Fruits that grow natural in the Countries are *Strawberries*, *Cramberries*, *Huckleberries*, *Blackberries*, *Mellers*, *Grapes*, *Plums*, *Hickery-Nuts*, *Walnuts*, *Mulberries*, *Chestnuts*, *Husselnuts*, *&c.*

Garden Fruits groweth well, as *Cabbage*, *Colworts*, *Colliflowers*, *Sparagrass*, *Carrots*, *Parsneps*, *Turnups*, *Oynions*, *Cowcumbers*, *Pumkins*, *Water-Mellons*, *Musk-Mellons*, *Squashes*, *Potatoes*, *Currants*, *Goosberries*, *Roses*, *Cornations*, *Tulips*, Garden-Herbs, Flowers. Seeds, Fruits, &c. for such as grow in *England*, certainly will grow here.

Orchards of *Apples*, *Pears*, *Quinces*, *Peaches*, *Aprecocks*, *Plums*, *Cheries*, and other sorts of the usual Fruits of *England* may be soon raised to good advantage, the Trees growing faster than in *England*, whereof great quantities of *Sider* may be made. And were Glass-houses erected to furnish us with Bottles, we might have a profitable Trade, by sending *Sider* to *Jamaica* and *Barbadoes*, &c. ready bottled, which is commonly so sent from *Herefordshire* to *London*.

It is supposed that we may make as good Wines as in *France*, (if Vineyards were planted on the sides of Hills or Banks, which are defended from the cold North-West Winds) with such Vines as the *French*-men commonly make those Wines of; for the Climate is as proper as any part of *France*, therefore it is rational to believe, that the Wines will be as rich and good as in *France*. There are some Vineyards already planted in *Pennsylvania*, and more intended to be planted by some *French-Protestants*, and others, that are gone to settle there. (See note No. 9).

Several other Commodities may be raised here, as *Rice* which is known to have been sown for a tryal, and it grew very well, and yielded good encrease.

Also *Annis-Seeds* I have been informed groweth well, and might be a profitable Commodity; there being great Quantities used in *England* by Distillers.

*Liquorish* doubtless would grow very well. And I question not but that *Mather*, *Woad*, and other Plants and Roots for Dyers use might be raised. *Shumuck* groweth naturally. Also several useful Drugs grow naturally, as *Sassafrass*, *Sassaperella*, *Callamus*, *Aromaticus*, *Snake-Root*, Iallappa, &c.

The *Pine-Tree* groweth here, out of which is made *Pitch*, *Tar*, *Rosin*, and Turpentine : In *New-England* some make quantities of *Tar* out of the knots of *Pine Trees*, with which they supply themselves and others.

There are many other sorts of *Plants*, *Roots* and Herbs of great Virtue, which grow here, which are found to cure such Distempers as the People are insident to.

*Hops* in some places grow naturally, but were *Hop-*Gardens planted in low rich Land, quantities might be raised to good advantage.

There is no *Lime Stone* as we yet know of, but we make *Lime* of *Oyster* Shels, which by the Sea and

Bay side are so plentiful, that we may load Ships with
them.

There are several sorts of good *Clay*, of which
Bricks, Earthen-Ware, and Tobacco-Pipes are made ;
and in some places there are Quaries of a ruf hard
Stone, which are good to wall Cellars, and some Stone
fit for Pavement.

The *Trees* grow but thin in most places, and very
little under-Wood. In the *Woods* groweth plentifully
a course sort of *Grass*, which is so proving that it soon
makes the Cattel and Horses fat in the Summer, but
the *Hay* being course, which is chiefly gotten on the
fresh Marshes, the Cattel loseth their Flesh in the
Winter, and become very poor, except we give them
Corn : But this may be remydied in time, by drain-
ing of low rich Land, and by plowing of it, and sow-
ing it with *English*-Grass-seed, which here thrives very
well.

The *Hogs* are fat in the Woods when it is a good
Mast-year.

The Woods are furnished with store of Wild Fowl,
as *Turkeys, Phesants, Heath-Cocks, Patridges, Pidgeons,
Blackbirds*, &c. And People that will take the pains
to raise the various sorts of tame Fowl, may do it with
as little trouble, and less charge, than they can in
*England*, by reason of what they find in the Woods.

*Bees* are found by the experience of several that
keep them, to thrive very well.

I do not question but that we might make good
strong sound *Beer*, *Ale* and *Mum*, that would keep well

to *Barbadoes* the Water being good, and *Wheat* and
*Barley* in a few Years like to be very plentiful : Great
quantities of *Beer*, *Ale* and *Mum* is sent yearly from
*London*, and other places, to *Barbadoes*, *Jamaica*, and
other Islands in *America*, where it sells to good advantage ; and if *Beer*, *Ale* and *Mum* (see note No. 10),
hold good from *England* to those places, which 'tis
said is above one thousand Leagues ; I question not
but if it be well brewed in a seasonable time of the
Year, and put up in good Casks, but it will keep good
to be Transported from *Delaware* River to those
Islands aforesaid, which by computation, is not above
half so far. If Merchants can gain by sending *Beer*,
*Ale* and *Mum* from *England*, where Corn is dear,
and Freight is dear, by reason of the length of the
Voyage, we in all probability must get much more,
that buy our Corn cheap, and pay less Freight.

*Flower* and *Bisket* may be made in great quantities
in a few Years, the Wheat being very good, which
seldom fails of finding a good Market at *Barbadoes*,
*Jamaica*, and the *Carib* Islands : great quantities are
sent yearly from London, and other places, which if
they can make Profit of it, we much more for the
Reasons already given.

*Pork* is but about half the price as in *England*,
therefore the Inhabitants will seldom have their
Market spoiled by any that come from *England*, of
which Commodity the Inhabitants in a few Years
will have Quantities to sell to the Merchant, which is
salted, and packed in Barrels, and so transported to

*Jamaica, Barbadoes, Nevis,* and other Islands. Hams
of *Bacon* are also made, much after the same manner
as in *West-Falia,* and the Bacon eats much like it.

Our *Beef* in the Fall is very fat and good, and we
are likely in a few Years to have great Plenty, which
will serve our Families, and furnish Shipping.

Our *Mutton* is also fat, sound and good being only
fed with natural Grass; but if we sprinkle but a little
*English* Hay-Seed on the Land without Plowing, and
then feed Sheep on it, in a little time it will so encrease, that it will cover the Land with *English* Grass,
like unto our Pastures in *England,* provided the Land
be good. We find the Profits of Sheep are considerable.

Our *Butter* is very good, and our *Cheese* is indifferent good, but when we have Pastures of *English* Grass,
(which many are getting into) then I suppose our
*Cheese* will be as good as that of *England.*

Our *Horses* are good serviceable Horses, fit both for
Draught and Saddle, the Planters will ride them fifty
Miles a day, without Shoes, and some of them are indifferent good shapes; of which many Ships are
freighted yearly from *New-England* with Horses to
*Barbadoes, Nevis,* and other places; and some Ships
have also been freighted out of *Pennsylvania* and *New-
Jersey* with Horses to *Barbadoes;* but if we had some
choise Horses from *England,* and did get some of the
best of our Mares, and keep them well in the Winter,
and in Pastures inclosed in the Summer, to prevent
there going amongst other Horses, we might then

have a choice breed of Horses, which would tend much to the advantage of the Inhabitants. (See note No. 11).

The Commodities fit to send to *England*, besides what are already named, are the Skins of the several wild Beasts that are in the Country, as *Elks, Deer, Beaver, Fisher, Bear, Fox, Rackoon, Marten, Otter, Woolf, Muskquash, Mink, Cat*, &c.

*Potashes* may be here made, and *Soap*, not only to the supply of our selves, but to sell to our Neighbours.

Also *Iron* may be here made, there being one *Iron-Work* already in East-*Jersey*. (See note No. 12).

Likewise, we may furnish Merchants with Pipe-Staves, and other Coopers Timber and Hoops.

The *Woolen* Manufacture may be mannaged in *Pennsylvania* and *New-Jersey*, to good advantage, the upper parts of the country being very fit for the keeping of Sheep, the Wool being found to be good, and the Sheep not subject to the *Rot:* The Ewes commonly after the first time, being two Lambs at once.

But it may be queried, *How shall the Sheep be preserved from the Woolf?*

I answer; Get such a Flock as it may answer the charge, for a boy to make it his full Employment to look after them, and let them be penned at Night in a House or Fold provided for that purpose. If one man have not enough to imploy a Shepherd, then let several joyn their Stock together.

But it may be queried, *Where shall Wool be gotten to*

*carry on the Woollen Manufacture, untill we have of our own raising?*

I answer; in *Road-Island*, and some other adjacent Islands and Places, Wool may be bought at six Pence a Pound, and considerable quantities may be there had, which will supply until we can raise enough of our own.

Also, we may have *Cotton*-Wool (see note No. 13) from *Barbadoes*, and other adjacent Islands in returns for our Provisions that we send them. So that the making of Cotton-Cloth and Fustians may be likewise made to good advantage, the *Cotton-Wool* being purchased by the growth of our own Country; and the Linnen-Yarn being spun by our own Families, of *Flax*, of our own growth and ordering.

The *Tanning*-Trade and *Shoemaking* may here be mannaged to good advantage, *Hides* being plenty, and to be had at moderate Prices, and *Bark* to be had for only the charge in getting it.

A *Skinner* that can dress Skins in Oyl, may do very well; for we have *Elk* skins, and plenty of *Buck* and *Doe* skins, which the Inhabitants give (at *New York*, where there are such Trades) one half for dressing the other.

There ought to be *publick Store-Houses* provided for all Persons to bring their Flax, Hemp and Linnen Cloth to, where it may be preserved clean and dry at a very small Charge, and the owner at liberty to take it out at his own will and pleasure, or to sell, transfer or assign it to another. Now the Hemp, Flax and Linnen Cloth being brought into the publick Store-

House, and the Quantity, Quality and Value of it there registred in the Book, to be kept for that purpose; and the Person that hath put in the said Hemp, Flax and Linnen Cloth, taking a Note under the Hand and Seal, from the Store-house Register, of the quantity, quality and value of the Hemp, Flax and Linnen Cloth, brought into the publick Store-House, with the time it was delivered; these Notes will pass from one man to another all one as Money: *As for Example,* Suppose I am a Merchant, that am furnished with divers sorts of goods, I sell them to a Planter, and receive their Notes which they had from the Store-house *Registry,* in pay for my goods, to the value of one hundred Pounds. I buy of the Clothier in Woolen Cloth to the value of sixty pounds, and of the Roper in Cordage to the value of forty pounds; I pay them by these Notes on the Store-house; the Clother he buys Woolen Yarn of the Master of the Spinning-School, to the value of sixty pounds, and payes him by these Notes on the publick Store; the Master of the Spinning-School buys of the Farmer in Wool to the value of sixty pounds, and pays him by these Notes; the Farmer buyeth of the Merchant in Goods to the value of sixty pounds, and pays him by these Notes; the Merchant receiveth on demand, from the publick Store, in Linnen Cloth to the value of sixty pound, at receiving thereof he delivereth up the Notes to the Register of the publick Store, which are cancelled, and then filed up as Waste paper. The

6

Roper, when he pleaseth, receives on demand, in
Hemp to the value of forty pounds out of the publick
Store, by which he is made capable of imploying his
Servants in making of Cordage; but he that hath no
occasion to take out this Hemp or Flax, or Linnen
Cloth, may pass these Notes from one man to another,
as often as they please, which is all one as ready
Money at all times.

Were the Flax and Hemp Manufacturies carried
on to that height as it might be, it would greatly
advance these Countries; for did we make our own
Sail-cloth and Cordage, we could make Ships, Sloops
and Boats at much easier Rates than they can build
for in *England*, the Timber costing us nothing but
Labour. And were more Saw-Mills made (see note No.
14) (of which there are divers already) to cut Planks
and other Timber, both Ships and Houses might be
built at easier Rates.

Many Ship Loads of Hemp is brought yearly from
the East Countries to *England*, which is afterward
there made into Cordage, Twine, Sacking, Fishing-
Nets &c. and then transported from thence to *Jamaica*,
*Barbadoes*, *Virginia*, *New-England*. and other parts of
*America*, so that doubtless materials made of Hemp,
must be sold in *America* by the Retailer, at double the
price as it cost where it grew; by which it appears
that at those prices we should have double for our
labour, to what they have, and our Provisions as Cheap
as theirs, it being raised on Land that cost us little.

1. Now It might be well if a Law were made by the Governours and general Assemblies of *Pennsylvania* and *New-Jersey*, that all Persons inhabiting in the said Provinces, do put their Children seven years to the publick School, or longer, if the Parents please. (See note No. 15).

2. That Schools be provided in all Towns and Cities, and persons of known honesty, skill and understanding be yearly chosen by the Governour and General Assembly, to teach and instruct Boys and Girls in all the most useful Arts and Sciences that they in their youthful capacities may be capable to understand, as the learning to *Read* and *Write true English, Latine*, and other useful Speeches and Languages, and *fair Writing, Arithmetick* and *Book-keeping*; and the Boys to be taught and instructed in some Mystery or Trade, as the making of *Mathematical Instruments, Joynery, Twinery*, the making of *Clocks* and *Watches, Weaving, Shoe-making*, or any other useful Trade or Mystery that the School is capable of teaching; and the Girls to be taught and instructed in *Spinning* of *Flax* and *Wool*, and *Knitting* of *Gloves* and Stockings, Sewing, and making of all sorts of useful *Needle-Work*, and the making of *Straw-Work*, as *Hats, Baskets*, &c. or any other useful Art or Mystery that the School is capable of teaching.

3. That the Scholars be kept in the Morning two hours at *Reading, Writing, Book-keeping*. &c. and other two hours at work in that Art, Mystery or Trade

339

that he or she most delighteth in, and then let them
have two hours to dine, and for Recreation ; and in the
afternoon two hours at *Reading, Writing, &c.* and the
other two hours at work at their several Imployments.

4. The seventh day of the Week the Scholars may
come to school only in the fore-noon, and at a certain
hour in the afternoon let a Meeting be kept by the
School-masters and their Scholars, where after good
instruction and admonition is given by the Masters,
to the Scholars and thanks returned to the Lord for
his Mercies and Blessings that are daily received from
him, then let a strict examination be made by the
Masters, of the Conversation of the Scholars in the
week past, and let reproof, admonition and correction
be given to the Offenders, according to the quantity
and quality of their faults.

5. Let the like Meetings be kept by the School-
Mistrisses, and the Girls apart from the Boys. By
strictly observing this good Order, our Children will
be hindred of running into that Excess of Riot and
Wickedness that youth is incident to, and they will
be a comfort to their tender Parents.

6. Let one thousand Acres of Land be given and
laid out in a good place, to every publick School that
shall be set up, and the Rent or income of it to go towards the defraying of the charge of the School.

7. And to the end that the Children of poor People,
and the Children of *Indians* may have the like good
Learning with the Children of Rich People, let them

340

be maintained free of charge to their Parents, out of the Profits of the school, arising by the Work of the Scholars, by which the Poor and the *Indians*, as well as the Rich, will have their children taught, and the Remainder of the Profits, if any be, to be disposed of in the building of School-houses, and Improvements on the thousand Acres of Land, which belongs to the School.

The manner and Profits of a Spinning-School in *Germany*, as it is laid down by *Andrew Yarenton* in his own words, in a Book of his, call'd, *England's Improvements by Sea and Land*, take as followeth.

'In *Germany*, where the Thred is made that
' makes the fine Linnens, in all Towns there are
' Schools for little Girls, six years old, and upwards, to
' teach them to spin, and so to bring their tender
' fingers by degrees to spin very fine ; their Wheels go
' all by the Foot, made to go with much ease, whereby
' the action or motion is very easie and delightful: The
' way, method, rule and order how they are govern'd
' is, 1st. There is a large Room, and in the middle
' thereof a little Box like a Pulpit: 2dly, There are
' Benches built round about the Room, as they are in
' Play-houses, upon the benches sit about two hun-
' dred Children spinning, and in the box in the middle
' of the Room, sits the grand Mistress with a long
' white Wand in her hand; if she observe any of them
' idle, she reaches them a tap, but if that will not do,
' she rings a bell, which by a little Cord is fixed to

' the box, and out comes a Woman, she then points to
' the Offendor. and she is taken away into another
' Room and chastized; and all this is done without
' one word speaking : In a little Room by the School
' there is a Woman that is preparing, and putting Flax
' on the Distaffs, and upon the ringing of a Bell, and
' pointing the Rod at the Maid that hath spun off her
' Flax, she hath another Distaff given her, and her
' Spool of Thred taken from her. and put into a box
' unto others of the same size. to make Cloth, all being
' of equal Threds.   1st. They raise their Children, as
' they spin finer, to the higher Benches : 2. They sort
' and size all the Threds. so that they can apply them
' to make equal Cloths ; and after a young Maid hath
' been three years in the *Spinning-School*, that is taken
' in at six. and then continues until nine years, she
' will get eight pence the day, and in these parts I
' speak of. a man that has most Children, lives best.

Now were Spinning-Schools settled in the principal
Cities and Towns in *Pennsylvania* and *New-Jersey*, and
a Law made to oblige the Parents of Children, to put
their Children to School, we should then soon come
into such a way of making Linnen-Cloth, as that we
should not only have sufficient for our own supply, but
also should have quantities to sell to the Inhabitants
of our own neighbouring Provinces, where it will sell
at considerable Prices, they being usually supplied from
*England*, where it must be dear, after Freight, Custom,
and other charges at Importation, with the Merchants

profit considered; and yet nevertheless this Cloth, thus dear bought will sell in *New-England, Virginia,* and some other places in *America,* at thirty Pound *per cent* profit, above the first cost in *England,* and the Moneys paid by Bills of Exchange, and the Retailer makes commonly on Goods thus bought not less than twenty Pounds *per cent.* profit: So that if all things be considered, the Cloth is sold in *America,* to the Planter at full double the price as it cost from the maker in *France* or *Germany,* from whence its brought to *England,* by which it doth appear, that if we do get such Prices for the Cloth that we make, then we shall have double for our Labour to what they have; therefore it may be well that a Law were made for the encouragement of the *Linnen Manufacture* by the Governours and General Assemblies, that all Persons inhabiting in *Pennsylvania,* or *New-Jersey,* that keep a Plow, do sow one Acre of *Flax,* and two Acres of *Hemp,* which would be a means of supplying us with *Flax* and *Hemp,* to carry on the Manufacturies of *Linnen-Cloth* and *Cordage;* and also would be very profitable to the Planter, by imploying his Family in the Winter season, when they would have otherwise but little else to do, *viz.* the Men and Boys in Breaking and Dressing of it, and making it fit for use, and the Women and Girls in Spinning it, and nevertheless they may carry on their Husbandry as largely, as if nothing of this was done; the Husbandry — Affairs being chiefly betwixt the Spring and Fall.

Now to that end that a *Bank* of *Monies* and *Credit* may be in *Pennsylvania* and *New-Jersey*, a Law may be made, that all Monies lent on Interest be at 8 l. *per cent.* by the year, and that all Bills and Bonds be entred on the publick Registry, and by Act of Assembly be made transferable by Assignments, so as the Property may go along with the Assignment; thereby a Bond or Bill will go in the Nature of *Bills of Exchange;* and so A. owing 200 l. to B. he assigns him the Bond of C. who owed him 200 l. and C. owing D. 200 l. assigns him the Bond of E. who owed him 200 l. and so one Bond or Bill would go through twenty hands, and thereby be as ready Monies, and do much to the Benefit of Trade. Also, that all Lands and Houses be put under a publick Registry, and entred in the Book, with an account of the value of them, and how occupied and tenanted, a particular thereof being given under the Hand and Seal of the Office to the Owners. We having thus fitted our selves with a publick Registry of all our Lands and Houses, whereby it is made ready Money at all times, without the charge of Law, or the necessity of a Lawyer; and a Law being made for the payment of such large Interest for Monies lent, and the security being so undeniably good, a Bank will in time arise, and such a Bank as will be for the Benefit and advantage of *Pennsilvania* and *New-Jersey*, and Trade universal. (See note No. 16).

Suppose myself, and some others have in Houses

and Lands in *Pennsilvania* or *New-Jersey,* worth 3000 l. and are minded to mannage and carry on the Linnen Manufacture, but cannot do it, without borrowing on Interest 2000 l. therefore we come to the Bank in *Pennsilvania* or *New-Jersey,* and there tender a particular of our Lands and Houses, and how occupied or tennanted, being worth 3000 l. in *Pennsilvania* or *New-Jersey,* and desire them to lend us 2000 l. and we will Mortgage our Land and Houses for it; the answer will be, *We will send to the Register's Office your particular, and at the return of the Messenger you shall have your answer:* The Registers send answer, it is our Lands and Houses, and occupied, and tenanted, and valued according to the particular, there needs no more words but to tell us the Money, with which we carry on the Trade briskly, to the great benefit and advantage of some hundreds of People that we set to work, and to the supplying of the Inhabitants with Cloth made of Flax, grown, drest, spun and wove in our own Provinces; which Trade we could not mannage and carry on without this credit, but having this credit, we go on with our Trade comfortably, and the Lender will have his ends answered, and his Moneys well secured. And its certain, such an Anchorage, Fund, and Foundation, will then bring out the Monyes unimployed from all Persons in these Provinces, even People of all degrees will put in their Monyes, which will be put out again into Trade to Merchants, and

7

such as stand in need of ready Monyes; and thereby
Trade is made easie, and much convenienced.

Suppose ten Families purchase in *Pennsilvania* or
*New-Jersey* five thousand Acres of Land, and they lay
out a small Township in the middle of it, for the
conveniency of neighbourhood, to each Family one
hundred Acres for Houses, Gardens, Orchards, Corn-
fields and Pastures of English Grass, the remainder to
lie in common, to feed their cattel; and suppose that
by that time they have built their dwelling Houses,
Cow-houses, Barns, and other Out-houses, and have
made Enclosures about their home-lots, that their
Monyes is all expended, and without a further
supply to buy Oxen and Horses to plow their Land,
and Cows to find their Families in Milk, Butter and
Cheese, and Sows to breed a stock on, they will live
but meanly for some time, therefore to amend their
condition they come to the Bank, and there tender
a particular of their Lands, valued to be worth 1500
l. on which they desire to take up 1000 l. to purchase a Stock of Oxen, Horses, Cows, Sows, Sheep
and Servants, by which they will be enabled to
carry on their Husbandry to great advantage, and
the benefit of the Province in general; and it may
be that in two or three years time, they may be
able to pay in this Money, with Interest. to the
owner; and in two or three years more may be able
to bring into the Bank, to be lent out to others, one
thousand pounds of their own Estates.

As to the benefit of **publick Granaries** on *Delaware River*, to keep the Corn for all Merchants, Bakers and Farmers that please to send it thither, that so the destruction and damages occasioned by Rats and Mice, may be prevented. In this Granary, Corn at all times may be taken in, from all Persons that please to send it, and the Corn so sent may be preserved sweet, safe, and in good Order, at a small charge for a whole year, and the owner at liberty to take it out at his own will and pleasure, or to sell, transfer or assign any part of the said Corn to any Person or Persons for the payment of his Debts, or to furnish himself with Clothing, or other Necessaries from the Merchant; and the Granary-keepers to give good security that all things should be faithfully done & discharged. Now the Corn being brought into the publick Granary, and there registered in the Register-Book, to be kept for that purpose; and the Person that hath put in said Corn, taking a Note under hand and seal, from the Granary-Register, of the quantity of Corn brought into the Granary, with the time it was delivered, and the matter and kind of the Corn, then these Advantages will ensue:

*First*, Preservation from the Rats and Mice, Straw to supply his Cattel, the Chaff for his Horses, and the light Corn to feed his Pigs and Poultry; his Husbandry mannaged with rule and order to his advantage; no forc'd haste, but thrashing and carrying the Corn to the Granary in times wherein his servants

have leisure; so in seeding time & harvest all People
are freed from that.   Besides, there being at all times
sufficient quantities of Corn in the Granaries to load
Ships, Merchants from *Barbadoes*, and other places,
will come to buy Corn; of one Farmer he may buy
one hundred Bushels. of another fifty, and so he may
buy the Corn that belongs to sixty or eighty Farmers,
and receive their Notes which they had from the
Granary-Office, which Corn he letteth lie in the
Granary until he have occasion to use it, then he
orders his Baker to go with those notes to the Granary-
Office, and receive such quantities as he hath a mind
shall be made into Flower and Bisket, which the
Baker does accordingly, and gets it packt up in Casks,
and sent to *Barbadoes*; the remainder. if he please, he
may sell to some other Merchant that lives at *Barbadoes*, or some other place, and when sold, may deliver
the said Merchant the Notes on the Granary-Office, at
sight whereof they may receive their Corn, if they
please, or they may pass those Notes from one to
another, as often as they please. which is all one as
Money, the Corn being lodged safe, and kept in the
publick Granary, will be the occasion of imploying
much of the Cash of *Pennsilvania* and *New-Jersey*;
most People near these publick Bank-Granaries, will
be dealing to have some Corn in Bank-Credit; for that
cannot miss of finding an encrease and benefit to them
in the rise of Corn.

    The best places at present for the building of

*Granaries*, are, 1 suppose, *Burlington* in *West-Jersey*, *Philadelphia* and *New-Castle* in *Pennsilvania*, and *New Perth* in *East-Jersey*, which places are excellently situated, there being many Navigable Rivers, whereby Trade is very communicable, and the Corn may be brought in Boats and Sloops from most places now inhabited, by water to these publick Granaries, for small charge, and from the Granaries may be carried to Water-Mills to grind, which are some of them so conveniently situated, that Boats may come to the Mill-Tayl, which is also a great conveniency to those that trade much in Corn.

Now I will demonstrate, and shew you the length, breadth and heighth the *Granaries* ought to be of, to hold this Corn; as also the Charge of building one of them, and the way how it should be built for the best advantage, with the way of ordering and managing the Corn, that it may keep good, sweet and clean, eight or ten years. The *Granaries* must be three hundred Foot long, eighteen Foot wide betwixt inside and inside, seven Stories high, each Story seven Foot high, all to be built of good well burnt Brick, and laid in Lime and Sand very well; the ends of the *Granaries* must be set *North* and *South*, so the sides will be *East* and *West;* and in the sides of the *Granaries*, there must be large Windows to open and shut close, that when the Wind blows at *West*, the Windows may be laid open, and then the *Granary* man will be turning and winding the Corn, and all Filth and

Dross will be blown out at the Window. When the
Weather is fair, then throw open the Windows, to let
in the Air to the Corn; and in the middle, there must
be Stoves to be kept with Fire in them in all moist or
wet times, or at going away of great *Frosts* and *Snow*,
to prevent moistness either in the Brick-walls, Timber,
Boards or Corn.    There must be in each side of the
*Granaries*, three or four long Troughs or Spouts fixt
in the uppermost Loft, which must run about twenty
Foot out of the Granary; and in fine Weather, the
*Granary* men must be throwing the Corn out of the
uppermost Loft, and so it will fall into another Spout
made ten Foot wide at the top, and through that
Spout the Corn descends into the lowermost Loft, and
then wound up on the inside of the Granary, by a
Crane fixt for that purpose, and the Corn receiving the
benefit of the Air, falling down thirty Foot before it
comes into the second Spout, cleanseth it from its filth
and Chaff; these Spouts are to be taken off and on, as
occasion requires, and to be fixt to another of the
Lofts, that when Vessels come to load Corn, they may
through these Spouts convey the Corn into the Boats
or Sloops, without any thing of Labour, by carrying it
on the Backs of men.

The charge of one *Granary* three Hundred Foot
long, eighteen Foot wide, seven Stories high, seven
Foot betwixt each story, being built with Brick in
*England*, as by the Account of *Andrew Yarenton*, take
as followeth; *Six hundred thousand of Bricks builds a*

Granary, *two Bricks and a half thick: the two first Stories, two Bricks thick the three next Stories, Brick and a half thick the two uppermost Stories; and the Brick will be made and delivered on the Place for eight Shillings the Thousand, the laying of Brick three Shillings the Thousand, Lime and Sand two Shillings the Thousand; so Brick-laying, Lime and Sand will be thirteen Shillings the Thousand, one hundred and fifty Tuns of Oak for Summers-Joists and Roof,* 170 l. *Boards for the six Stories, sixty thousand Foot, at* 13s. 4d. *The one hundred Foot and ten thousand Foot for Window-Doors and Spouts at the same rate,* 48 l. *Laths and Tiles* 100 l. *Carpenters work* 70 l. Iron, Nails and odd things 60 l. *So the charge of a Granary will be* 800 l. *There will be kept in this* Granary *fourteen thousand Quarters of Corn, which is two thousand Quarters in every Loft, which will be a thousand Bushels in every Bay; six labouring men, with one Clerk, will be sufficient to manage this* Granary, *to turn and wind the Corn, and keep the Books of Accounts; fifteen pounds a piece allowed to the six men, and thirty pound a year to the Clerk and Register, will be Wages sufficient; so the Servants Wages will be* 120 l. per annum, *allow ten in the hundred for Monies laid out for building the* Granaries, *which is* 80 l. *so the charge will be yearly* 200 l. *Now if the Country-man pay six pence a Quarter yearly for keeping his Corn safe and sweet in the Granary, fourteen thousand Quarters will come to* 350 l. *for Granary-Rent yearly.*

Admit I have a Propriety of Land in *Pennsilvania* or *New-Jersey*, either place then alloweth me to take up five thousand Acres, with Town or City-Lots, upon condition that I settle ten Families on it, therefore I send over ten Families of honest industrious People, the charge of each Family is 100 l. as by the account of particulars appears, as followeth.

|  | l. | s. | d. |
|---|---|---|---|
| For one hundred Acres of Land     - | 05 | 00 | 00 |
| For the Passage of the Family, five persons,     -     -     -     -     -     - | 25 | 00 | 00 |
| For fresh provisions to use on Shipboard, over and above the Ships allowance, as *Rice. Oatmeal, Flower. Butter, Sugar, Brandy*, and some odd things more, which I leave to the discretion of those that go,     -     -     -     -     - | 05 | 00 | 00 |
| For 3 hundred weight of six penny, eight penny and ten penny Nails, to be used on sides and Roof of the House.  - | 05 | 00 | 00 |
| For a Share and Coulter, a Plow-Chain, 2 Scythes, 4 Sickles, a horse Collar, some Cordage for Harness, 2 Stock Locks, 2 weeding Hoes, 2 grubbing Hoes, one cross-cut Saw, 2 Iron Wedges, 1 Iron Pot, 1 frying Pan, 2 falling Axes, 1 broad Ax, 1 Spade, 1 Hatchet, 1 Fro to cleave Clapboard, Shingle and Coopers Timber,     -     - | 05 | 00 | 00 |

| | l. | s. | d. |
|---|---|---|---|
| For Portridge, Custom-house charge and freight, &c. on the goods,   -    - | 02 | 00 | 00 |
| For Insurance of the one hundred pound   -   -   -   -   -   - | 03 | 00 | 00 |
| In all -   -   - | 50 | 00 | 00 |

The remaining fifty Pounds may do well to lay out in these goods, which are the most vendable in the Country, *viz.*

| | l. | s. | d. |
|---|---|---|---|
| Ten pieces of Serge, at  -   -   - | 20 | 00 | 00 |
| Six pieces of narrow blew Linnen, containing about two hundred Yards, - | 05 | 00 | 00 |
| 200 Els of brown Ossembrigs, at about  -  -  -  -  -  - | 07 | 10 | 00 |
| Half a piece of three quarters Dowlis, | 03 | 10 | 00 |
| Three pieces of coulered Linnen  - | 02 | 10 | 00 |
| Two pieces of Yorkshire Kerseys,  - | 04 | 00 | 00 |
| One piece of red Peniston, above 40 yards, at 18 d, *per* Yard,  -  -  - | 03 | 00 | 00 |
| One piece of Demity,  -   -   - | 00 | 15 | 00 |
| In Buttons and Silk, Tape and Thred suitable to the Clothes,  -   - | 03 | 15 | 00 |
| In All   -   - | 50 | 00 | 00 |

And when you come into the Country, you may lay out the above-mentioned goods to purchase a stock of Cattel and Provisions, *&c.* which for goods at the first cost in *England*, will buy at the prices under-mentioned, *viz.*

8

|                                                                      | l.  | s.  | d.  |
|----------------------------------------------------------------------|-----|-----|-----|
| One pair of working Oxen. at          -                              | 06  | 00  | 00  |
| One Mare 3 l. and four Cows and Calves, 12 l.     -    -    -    -    | 15  | 00  | 00  |
| One Bull 2 l. ten Ewes 3 l. 10 s.         -                          | 05  | 10  | 00  |
| Four breeding Sows, and one Boor, -                                  | 04  | 00  | 00  |
| One fat Ox to kill for winter Provisions, -    -    -    -    -    -  | 03  | 10  | 00  |
| 400 pound of Pork, at 3 half pence per pound,    -    -    -    -     | 02  | 10  | 00  |
| 24 pound of Butter, at 4 d. per pound,                               | 00  | 08  | 00  |
| One Barrel of salted Fish,         -    -                            | 00  | 10  | 00  |
| One Barrel of Malassas to make Beer,                                 | 01  | 08  | 00  |
| 40 Bushels of Indian Corn, at 1 s. 8 d. per Bushel,  -    -    -    - | 03  | 06  | 08  |
| 20 Bushels of Rye, at 2 s. per Bushel,                               | 02  | 00  | 00  |
| 20 Bushels of Wheat, at 3 s. per Bushel,                             | 03  | 00  | 00  |
| 6 Bushels of Pease and Indian Beans, at 3 s. per Bushel.    -    -   | 00  | 18  | 00  |
| 2 Bushels of Salt, at 2 s. per Bushel, -                             | 00  | 04  | 00  |
| 50 pound of Cheese of the Country-making. at 3 d. per pound,  -  -   | 00  | 12  | 06  |
| 12 pound of Candles. at 5 d. per pound,                              | 00  | 05  | 00  |
| In Sugar, Spice, and other things.   -                               | 00  | 17  | 10  |
| In All        -    -                                                 | 50  | 00  | 00  |

Note, That the above-mentioned Prices is for goods
at first cost in England, which in Country Money

would be something above one third higher, *viz*. a Cow
and Calf valued in goods at first cost at 3 d. is worth
in Country Money 5 l. and other things advance much
after the same proportion.

My five thousand Acres of Land cost me 100 l. I
had of the ten Families for the one thousand Acres
disposed of to them 50 l. my Town or City Lots will
yield me currant 50 l. by which it appears I am nothing out on the four thousand Acres that is left.

I get my five thousand Acres surveyed and laid out
to me, out of which I lay out for the ten Families one
thousand Acres, which may be so divided, as that each
family may live near one to the other; I indent
with them to let the Money lie in their hands six
years, for which they to pay me each family, 8 l. a
year, in consideration of the one hundred pound a
family laid out for them, and at the expiration of the
six years, they to pay me my 1000 l. viz. each family
100 l. as by agreement; my Money being paid me, I
am unwilling to let it lie dead, therefore I lay out in
the middle of my Land one thousand Acres, which I
divide into ten lots, in form and manner as before,
then I indent, with fifty servants to serve me four
years a piece, I place them on the Land. *viz*. five on
each lot. Their Passage, and in goods to purchase
Cattel and Provisions, &c. is to each five servants
100 l. as before is explained; Now I order a House to
be built, and Orchards, Gardens and Inclosures to be

made, and Husbandry affairs to be carried on on each
lot; so that at the four years end, as the servants
time is expired, I shall have ten Farms, each containing four hundred Acres; for the one thousand Acres
being laid out in the middle of my Land, the remaining three thousand Acres joyns to it.

My servants time being expired, I am willing to
see what charge I am out upon these ten Farms and
Stock, in order to know what I have gain'd in the ten
years past, over and above 8 *l.* *per* *Cent.* *Interest,* that
is allowed me for the use of my Money : I am out by
the first charge 1000 l. & the Interest thereof for four
years, at 8 *l.* *per* *Cent.* is for the four years 320 l. so
that the whole charge on the ten Farms, Principal
& Interest, comes to 1320 l. Now if I value my ten
Farms but at 400 l. each, which is 20 *s.* *per* *Acre,* one
with another; then the whole will be 4000 l. besides
the first Stock of Cattel and Hogs. &c. to each Plantation. with its Increase for four years, which Stock cost
at first to each Farm 30 l. in goods at first cost. but is
worth 40 l. sterling, at which rate the Stock on the
ten Farms cost 400 l. and if we account the four years
Increase to be no more than the first Stock. yet that is
400 l. by which it appears that the ten Farms, and the
stock on them is worth 4800 l. out of which deduct
the Money laid out. which with Interest is 1320 l. So
that the Neat profit. besides 8 l. *per* *Cent.* allowed for
Interest, is for this ten years improvement, 3480 l. and
twenty Families set at liberty from that extream

Slavery that attended them, by reason of great Poverty that they endured in *England*, and must have so continued, had not they been thus redeemed by coming into *America*. It may be thought that this is too great an undertaking for one man, which if it be, then I propose that ten joyn together in this community, and each man send over five Servants, of which let one of them be an honest man that understands Country business, as an Overseer, which if we allow him over and above his Passage and Diet 20 l. a year for his four years service, this amounts to 80 l. which is for the ten farms 800 l. which being deducted out of the 3480 l. there only remains 2680 l. clear profit to the ten men, which is for each man 268 l. for his ten years improvement of his 100 l. and his 100 l. back again with Interest for all the time at 8 l. *per Cent. per annum*, the whole producing 448 l. for his 100 l. first laid out.

Some may object, and say, *They cannot believe the Land of each farm, with its Improvements, will sell at 20 s. an Acre, that is, at twelve years purchase* is 1 s. 8 d. per Acre per annum, *because three hundred Acres of it is as it was*, viz. *Rough Woods.*

I *Answer;* That although it be so, yet these Woods are made valuable by the twenty Families that are seated near them, the first ten families having been settled ten years, the last four years; for some are willing to have their children live near them; and they having but one hundred Acres in all, it will not be well to divide that, therefore they will give a good

price for one hundred Acres, to settle a Child upon, to
live by them, as experience sheweth; for in *Rhode-
Island*, which is not far from us, Land rough in the
Woods, not better than ours, will sell at 40 s. an Acre,
which is 3 *s.* 4 *d. per Acre per annum*. Therefore,
Reader, I hope now thou art convinced that there is a
probability that what I here inform thee of, will prove
true, casualties of Fire, &c. excepted.

The *Indians* are but few in Number, and have been
very serviceable to us by selling us Venison, *Indian*
Corn, Pease and Beans, Fish and Fowl, *Buck* Skins,
*Beaver*, *Otter*, and other Skins and Furs; the Men
hunt, Fish and Fowl, and the Women plant the Corn,
and carry Burthens: they are many of them of a good
Understanding, considering their education; and in
their publick meetings of Business, they have excellent Order, one speaking after another, and while one
is speaking all the rest keep silent, and do not so much
as whisper one to the other: We had several Meetings
with them, one was in order to put down the sale of
*Rum*, *Brandy*, and other strong Liquors to them, they
being a People that have not Government of themselves, so as to drink it in moderation: at which time
there were eight Kings, (& many other *Indians*) one
of them was *Ockanickon*, whose dying Words I writ
from his Mouth, which you shall have in its order.

The *Indian* Kings sate on a Form, and we sate on
another over against them: they had prepared four

Belts of *Wampum*, (See note No. 17) (so their current Money is called, being Black and White *Beads* made of a Fish Shell) to give us as Seals of the Covenant they made with us; one of the Kings by the consent and appointment of the rest stood up and made this following Speech; *The strong Liquors was first sold us by the* Dutch, *and they were blind, they had no Eyes, they did not see that it was for our hurt ; and the next People that came amongst us, were the* Sweeds, *who continued the sale of those strong Liquors to us : they were also Blind, they had no Eyes, they did not see it to be hurtful to us to drink it, although we know it to be hurtful to us ; but if People will sell it us, we are so in love with it, that we cannot forbear it ; when we drink it, it makes us mad ; we do not know what we do, we then abuse one another ; we throw each other into the Fire, seven Score of our People have been killed, by reason of the drinking of it, since the time it was first sold us : Those People that sell it, they are blind, they have no Eyes, but now there is a People come to live amongst us, that have Eyes, they see it to be for our Hurt, and we know it to be for our Hurt : They are willing to deny themselves of the Profit of it if for our good ; these People have Eyes ; we are glad such a People are come amongst us. We must put it down by mutual consent ; the Cask must be sealed up, it must be made fast, it must not leak by Day nor by Night, in the Light, nor in the Dark, and we give you these four Belts of* Wampam, *which we would have you lay up safe, and keep by you to be Witness of this Agree-*

*ment that we make with you, and we would have you tell your Children, that these four Belts of* Wampam *are given you to be Witness betwixt us and you of this Agreement.*

---

*A Letter from* New-Jersey *in* America *to a Friend in* London.

Dear Friend;

I Having this short oppertunity, have nothing to present thee with. but the Dying-Words of an *Indian* King, who died in *Burlington,* and was buried amongst Friends according to his desire; and at his Burial many Tears were shed both by the *Indians* and *English;* so in Love, and great haste, I rest thy Friend,

John Cripps. (See note No. 18).

---

*The Dying-Words of* Ockanichon. *spoken to* Jachkursoe, *whom he appointed King after him, spoken in the Presence of several, who were Eye and Ear Witnesses of the Truth thereof.*

IT was my desire, that my Brother's Son, *Jahkursoe* should be sent for to come to hear my last Words, whom I have appointed King after me. My Brother's Son, this day I deliver my Heart into thy Bosom, and would have thee love that which is Good and to keep good Company, and to refuse that which is Evil; and

360

to avoid bad Company. Now inasmuch as I have
delivered my Heart into thy Bosom I also deliver my
Bosom to keep my Heart therein; therefore alwayes
be sure to walk in a good Path, and never depart out
of it. And if any Indians should speak any evil of
*Indians* or *Christians*, do not joyn with it, but to look
to that which is Good, and to joyn with the same
alwayes. Look at the Sun from the Rising of it to
the Setting of the same. In Speeches that shall be
made between the *Indians* and *Christians*, if any thing
be spoke that is evil, do not joyn with that, but joyn
with that which is good; and when Speeches are made,
do not thou speak first, but let all speak before thee, and
take good notice what each man speaks, and when thou
hast heard all, joyn to that which is good. Brother's
Son, I would have thee to cleanse thy Ears, and take
all Darkness and Foulness out, that thou mayst take
notice of that which is Good and Evil, and then to
joyn with that which is Good, and refuse the Evil;
and also to cleanse thy Eyes, that thou mayest see
both Good and Evil; and if thou see any Evil, do not
joyn with it, but joyn to that which is Good. Brother's Son, Thou has heard all that is past; now I would
have thee to stand up in time of *Speeches*, and to stand
in my *Steps*, and follow my *Speeches* as I have said
before thee, then what thou dost desire in Reason will
be granted thee. Why shouldst thou not follow my
Example, inasmuch as I have had a mind to do that

9

which is Good, and therefore do thou also the same?
Whereas *Schoppy* and *Swanpis* were appointed Kings
by me in my stead, and I understanding by my Doctor,
that *Schoppy* secretly advised him not to cure me, and
they both being with me at *John Hollinshead's* House,
there I my self see by them that they were given more
to *Drink*, than to take notice of my *last Words*, for I
had a mind to make a Speech to them, and to my
Brethren the *English Commissioners*, therefore I refused
them to be Kings after me in my stead, and have
chosen my Brother's Son *Iahkurosoe* in their stead to
succeed me.

Brother's Son, I desire thee to be plain and fair with
all, both *Indians* and *Christians*, as I have been. I
am very weak, otherwise I would have spoken more;
and in Testimony of the Truth of this, I have hereunto set my Hand.

The mark ⌊ of *Ockanickon*, King, now deceased.

*Henry Jacob Falckinbery*, Intrepreter.

*Friendly Reader*, when *Ockanickon* had given his
Brothers Son this good Counsel, I thought meet to
speak unto him as followeth; *There is a great God, who
created all things, and this God giveth Man an understanding of what is Good, and what is Bad, and after
th Life rewardeth the Good with Blessings, and the Bad
according to their Doings ;* to which he answered and
said, *It is very true, it is so, there are two Wayes, a broad
Way, and a strait Way; there be two Paths, a broad*

302

*Path and a strait Path ;* the worst, and *the greatest Number go in the broad Path, the best and fewest go in the strait Path.* T. B.

---

*Something in Relation to a Conference had with the* Indians *at* Burlington, *shortly after we came into the Country.*

THE *Indians* told us, they were advised to make War on us, and cut us off whilst we were but few, and said, They were told, that we sold them the *Small-Pox*, with the Mach Coat they had bought of us, which caused our People to be in Fears and Jealousies concerning them ; therefore we sent for the *Indian* Kings, to speak with them, who with many more *Indians*, came to *Burlington*, where we had Conference with them about the matter, therefore told them, That we came amongst them by their own consent, and had bought the Land of them, for which we had honestly paid them for, and for what Commodities we had bought at any time of them, we had paid them for, and had been just to them, and had been from the time of our first coming very kind and respectful to them, therefore we knew no Reason that they had to make War on us; to which one of them, in the behalf of the rest, made this following Speech in answer, saying, 'Our Young Men may speak such 'Words as we do not like, nor approve of, and we can-

'not help that: And some of your Young Men may
'speak such Words as you do not like. and you cannot
'help that. We are your Brothers, and intend to live
'like Brothers with you: We have no mind to have
'War. for when we have War, we are only Skin and
'Bones; the Meat that we eat doth not do us good,
'we alwayes are in fear. we have not the benefit of
'the Sun to shine on us. we hide us in Holes and
'Corners; we are minded to live at Peace: If we
'intend at any time to make War upon you. we will
'let you know of it, and the Reasons why we make
'War with you; and if you make us satisfaction for
'the Injury done us, for which the War is intended,
'then we will not make War on you. And if you
'intend at any time to make War on us. we would
'have you let us know of it, and the Reasons for which
'you make War on us, and then if we do not make
'satisfaction for the Injury done unto you, then you
'may make War on us, otherwise you ought not to do
'it. You are our Brothers. and we are willing to live
'like Brothers with you: We are willing to have a
'*broad Path* for you and us to walk in. and if an *Indian*
'is asleep in this *Path*. the *English*-man shall pass him
'by, and do him no harm; and if an *English*-man is
'asleep in this *path*, the *Indian* shall pass him by, and
'say, *He is an English-man he is asleep. let him alone,*
'*he loves to Sleep.* It shall be a *plain Path*, there must
'not be in this *path* a *stump* to hurt our *feet*. And as

'to the *Small-Pox*, it was once in my *Grandfathers*
'time, and it could not be the *English* that could send
'it us then, there being no *English* in the Country, and
'it was once in my *Fathers* time, they could not send it
'us then neither; and now it is in my time, I do not
'believe that they have sent it us now: I do believe it
'is the Man above that hath sent it us.

Some are apt to ask, How we can propose safely to
live amongst such a Heathen People as the Indians,
whose Principles and Practices leads them to War and
Bloodshed, and our Principles and Practices leading
us to love Enemies, and if reviled, not to revile again;
and if smitten on the one cheek to turn the other, and
we being a peaceable People, whose Principles and
Practices are against Wars and Fightings?

I *Answer:* That we settled by the Indians consent
and good liking, and bought the Land of them, that
we settle on, which they conveyed to us by Deed under
their Hands and Seals, and also submitted to several
Articles of agreement with us, viz. **Not to do us
any Injury;** but if it should so happen, that any
of their People at any time should injure or do harm
to any of us, then they to make us satisfaction for the
Injury done; therefore if they break these Covenants
and Agreements, then they may be proceeded against
as other Offendors, *viz.* to be kept in subjection to the
Magistrates Power, in whose hand the Sword of Justice is committed to be used by him, for the punish-

ment of Evil-doers, and praise of them that do well; therefore I do believe it to be both lawful and expedient to bring Offendors to Justice by the power of the Magistrates Sword, which is not to be used in vain, but may be used against such as raise Rebellions and Insurrections against the Government of the Country, be they *Indians* or others, otherwise it is in vain for us to pretend to Magistracy or Government, it being that which we own to be lawful both in Principle and Practice.

Q. Whether there be not Bears, Wolves, and other Ravenous Beasts in the Country?

I *Answer:* Yes. But I have travell'd alone in the Country some hundreds of Miles, and by missing of my way have lain in the Woods all night, and yet I never saw any of those Creatures, nor have I heard that ever man, woman or child were hurt by them, they being afraid of Mankind; also, encouragement is given to both *Indians* and others to kill Wolves, they being paid for every Wolfs head that they bring to the Magistrate, the value of ten Shillings; and the Bears the *Indians* kill for the profit of their Skins, and sake of their Flesh, which they eat, and esteem better than Deers flesh.

Q. Whether there be not Snakes, more especially the Rattle-Snake?

*Ans.* Yes, but not many Rattle-Snakes, and they are easily discovered; for they commonly lie in the

Paths for the benefit of the Sun, & if any Person draws nigh them, they shake their Tail, on which the Rattles grow, which make a noise like a childs Rattle; I never heard of but one Person bitten in *Pennsilvania* or *New-Jersey* with the Rattle-Snake, and he was helpt of it by live Chickens slit assunder and apply'd to the place, which drew out the Poyson; and as to the other Snake, the most plentiful is a black Snake, its bite, 'tis said, does no more harm than the prick of a Pin.

I have mentioned before, that there are a sort of troublesom Flies call'd *Musketoes* (much like the Gnats in *England*) in the lower parts of the Country, where the great Marshes are, but in the upper parts of the Country seldom one is seen.

There are Crows and Black birds, which may be accounted amongst the inconveniences, they being destructive to the *Indian Corn*, the Crows by picking up the Corn just as its appearing in the blade above ground, and the Black-birds by eating it in the Year, before it be full hard, if not prevented by looking after; but other sorts of Corn they seldom hurt.

It is rational to believe, that all considerate Persons will sit down and count the cost before they begin to build; for they must expect to pass through a Winter before a Summer, but not so troublesom a Winter as many have imagined; for those that come there to settle now, may purchase Corn, Cattel, and other

things at the prices mentioned, and many have Houses
in some of the Towns of *Pennsilvania* and *New-Jersey*
on Rent, until they build for themselves, and Water-
Mills to grind their Corn, which are such Conveniences
that we that went first partly missed of.

*Thus,* Kind Reader, I *have given thee a true Description of* Pennsilvania *and* New-Jersey, *with the* Rivers
*and* Springs, Fish *and* Fowle. Beasts. Fruits, Plants,
Corn *and* Commodities *that it doth or may produce, with
several other things needful for thee to know, as well* Inconveniences *as* Conveniences, *by which* I keep *clear of
that just Reflection of such as are more apt to see faults
in others, than to amend them in themselves.*

T. B.

Whereas I unavisedly published in Print a *Paper*
(see note No. 19), dated the 13th of *July,* 1685,
entituled, A *true and perfect Account of the disposal of the
one hundred Shares or Proprieties of the Province of West*
New-Jersey, *by* Edward Bylling: In which *Paper* I
gave an Account of the purchasers Names, and the
several Proprieties granted to them, part of which I
took from the Register, the remainder from a List
given in by *Edward Bylling,* to the Proprioters, as
mentioned on the said *Paper,* which *Paper* I find hath
proved Injurious to the aforesaid *Edward Bylling,*
although not so intended by me. Therefore in order

to give him Satisfaction, and all others that are concerned, I do acknowledge he hath, since the publishing of that *Paper*, shewed me some Deeds, wherein he hath several Proprieties conveyed back to him again, from the original Purchasers and Judge, he may make good Titles to the same.

—

A *Letter by* Thomas Budd, *sent to his Friends in* Pennsilvania *and* New-Jersey.

*Dear Friends;*

YOu are often in my Remembrance, and at this time I feel the tender Bowels of our heavenly Father's Love flowing in my Heart towards you, in a sence of those great Exercises that many of you have, do and may meet withal in your *Spiritual Travel* towards the *Land of Promise.*

I am also sensible of the many *Exercises* and inward *Combats* that many of you met withal. after you felt an inclination in your Hearts of Transplanting your selves into *America:* Oh the *Breathings* and fervent *Prayers*, and earnest *Desires* that were in your Hearts to the Lord, *That you might not go except it was his good Pleasure to remove you, for a purpose of his own:* This you earnestly desired to be satisfied in, and many of you received satisfaction. that it was your places to

10

leave your Native Country, Trades, and near and dear
Relations and Friends to transplant your selves into
a Wilderness. where you expected to meet with many
Tryals and Exercises of a differing kind, than what
you had met withal in your Native Country; but
this you contentedly gave up to, but not without
earnest desire. and fervent Prayers to the Lord for his
Wisdom to govern you, and his Fatherly Care to preserve you. and his comfortable presence to be with you,
to strengthen and enable you chearfuly to undergo
those new and unaccustomed Tryals and Exercises,
that you were sensible would attend you in this
weighty undertaking, the Lord heard your Prayers,
and answered your Desires, inasmuch as that his
Fatherly Care was over you, and his living Presence
did accompany you over the great Deep; so that you
saw his wonderful Deliverence, and in a sence thereof,
you praised his Name for the same.

The Lord having thus far answered our Souls desire,
as to bring us to our desired Port in safety, and to
remain with us, to be a Counsellor of good things unto
us, let us now answer this Kindness unto us by a
*righteous Conversation*, and a *pure*, *holy* and *innocent
Life*, that others beholding the same, may be convinced
thereby, and may glorifie our heavenly Father.

The Eyes of many are on us. some for Good, and
some for Evil; therefore my earnest Prayers are to
the Lord, That he would preserve us, and give us *Wis-*

*dom*, that we may be governed aright before him, and that he would give a good Understanding to those that are in Authority amongst us, that his Law may go forth of *Sion*, and his Word from *Jerusalem:* Be not backward in discharging that great Trust committed to you in your respective Offices and Places, that you may be help-meets in the Restoration.

And be careful to suppress, and keep down all Vice, and disorderly Spirits, and incourage Virtue, not only in the general, but every one in his perticular Family; there is an incumbant Duty lieth on all Masters of Families over their Family, therefore my desire is, that we may call our Families together at convenient times and Seasons, to wait upon the Lord, and to seek to him for *Wisdom* and *Counsel*, that his Blessings may attend us and our Families, and our Children may sit about our Table as Olive-branches full of Virtue, then shall we be full of Joy and Peace, and living Praises will spring to the Lord, in that his Blessings and Fatherly Care hath been thus continued towards us.

*Dear Friends;* be tender and helpful one towards another, that the Lord may bless and fill you with his divine Love, and sweet refreshing Life, which unities our Souls to each other, and makes us as one Family of Love together : Let us not entertain any hard Thoughts one of another, but if difference should happen amongst us, let a speedy and peaceable end be put unto it; for if Prejudices enter, it will eat out the

precious Life, and make us barren and unfruitful to
God.   We are not without our daily Exercises, Travels
and Temptations, therefore do desire the Lord may
put it into your Hearts, to Pray for our Preservation,
and our safe return to you, that we may meet together
again in the same overcoming Love of God, in which
we parted from you.

My Heart is full of Love to you, and do long to see
your Faces, and to enjoy your Company, that I may
more fully express that pure Love of God that springs
in my Heart unto you, then I can do by Writing.
Therefore I desire you may rest satisfied with these
few Lines, and receive them as a token of unfeigned
Love.   From

Your dear Friend,

Thomas Budd.

London, the 29th ⎫
   of the 8th      ⎬
   Month, 1684.   ⎭

Some material Things omitted in the foregoing part.

IT is to be noted, that the Tide runs to the Falls of
    *Delaware*, it being one hundred and fifty Miles
from the Capes, or entrance of the said River (which
Falls, is a ledge of Rocks lying a cross the River) and
also it runs up in some of the Cricks, ten or fifteen
Miles, the said River and Cricks being navigable for

Ships of great Burthen, there having lain over against *Burlington*, a Ship of about the burthen of four hundred Tuns afloat in four Fathom, at dead low Water, and the Flood riseth six or eight Foot; and there being no Worm that eats the bottoms of the Ships, as is usually done in *Virginia* and *Barbadoes*, &c. which renders the said Countries very fit for Trade and Navigation; And in the said River and Cricks are many other sorts of good *Fish*, not already named, some of which are *Cut-fish, Trout, Eales, Pearch*, &c.

## FINIS.

# NOTES.

### Note 1, page 27.

Budd's treatise was, perhaps, the most thorough attempt that had as yet been made, to call the attention of his countrymen to the advantages of a settlement in the then almost wilderness region of Pennsylvania and New Jersey, and the writer, it will be found, brought to the undertaking, a liberal and enlightened spirit, no small share of knowledge and sagacity, and the experience of many years' residence in the new country.

### Note 2, page 27.

Our author, so far as relates to New Jersey, refers to Item 7 of the Concession and Agreement, of 1664, of Berkeley and Carteret. "That no person qualified as aforesaid (that is either a subject of the king of England, or who shall become such) within the said province, at any time, shall be any ways molested, punished, disquieted, or called in question, for any difference in opinion or practice in matters of religious concernments, who does not actually disturb the civil peace of the said province; but that all and every such person and persons, may from time to time and at all times, freely and fully have and enjoy his and their judgment and consciences, in matters of religion throughout the said province, they behaving themselves peaceably and quietly, and not using this liberty to licentiousness, nor to the civil injury or outward disturbance of others; any law statute or clause contained or to be contained, usage or custom of this realm of England to the contrary thereof in any wise notwithstanding."

The language of the xvi chapter "of the Charter or fundamental laws of West New Jersey, agreed upon " in 1676, is still more emphatic and comprehensive, and breathes the spirit of men who had suffered for conscience sake.

"That no men, *nor number of men upon earth*, hath power or authority to rule over men's consciences in religious matters; therefore it is consented, agreed and ordained that no person or persons whatsoever, within

375

the said province, at any time or times hereafter, shall be any ways, upon any pretense whatsoever, called in question, or in the least punished or hurt, either in person estate or privilege, for the sake of his opinion, judgment, faith or worship towards God in matters of religion : but that all and every such person and persons. may from time to time, and at all times, freely and fully have and enjoy his and their judgments, and the exercise of their consciences. in matters of religious worship throughout all the said province."— Smith's *History of New Jersey.* 513, 520.

Also see the 10th article of the proposals agreed upon the 9th Nov., 1681, by Gov. Jenings and the Assembly. *Id.*, 128.

The same principles are asserted in the Laws agreed upon in England, on the 5th May, 1682, between Penn and the future freemen of his Province.

Law 35th. "That all persons living in this province who confess and acknowledge the one almighty and eternal God, to be the creator, upholder and ruler of the world, and that hold themselves obliged in conscience to live peaceably and justly in civil society, shall in no ways be molested or prejudiced for their religious persuasion or practice in matters of faith and worship, nor shall they be compelled at any time to frequent or maintain any religious worship, place or ministry whatever."

### Note 3, page 29.

Our author's account shows less change in the temperature of the region he describes, than is generally attributed to it.

For a description equally interesting and instructive. see Surveyor Colden's narrative of the temperature and climate of the same territory, written in 1723.—*Documents relating to the Colonial History of New York,* edited by Dr. O'Callaghan. V, 680.

The reader is also referred to the statements of Thomas Rudyard, Samuel Groome, Gawen Lawrie and others, in Smith's *New Jersey*, 167 to 189.

### Note 4, page 29.

"When the Yorkshire commissioners found the others were like to settle at such a distance, they told them if they would agree to fix by them. they would join in settling a town and that they should have the largest share, on consideration that they ( the Yorkshire commissioners ) had the best land in the woods: Being few, and the Indians numerous, they agreed to it.

"The commissioners employed Noble, a surveyor, who came in the first ship, to divide the spot. After the main street was ascertained, he divided the land on each side into lots; the easternmost among the Yorkshire proprietors, the other among the Londoners: To begin a settlement ten lots, of nine acres each, bounding on the west were laid out; that done some passengers from Wicknco, chiefly those concerned in the Yorkshire tenth, arrived the latter end of October. The London commissioners employed Noble to divide the part of the island yet unsurveyed, between the ten London proprietors, in the manner before mentioned: The town thus by mutual consent laid out, the commissioners gave it the name first of New Beverley, then Bridlington, but soon changed it to Burlington."— Smith's *History of New Jersey*, 98, 104.

Beverley was a town in Yorkshire, England, as was Burlington. The latter is styled "Burlington *or* Bridlington," a seaport town of England in the East Riding of Yorkshire, situated on a bay called Burlington Bay, formed by Flamborough Head, which is about 5 miles distant, nearly N. E. Considerable trade is carried on here; and that part of it called Burlington Quay, which is built on the coast, a mile from the town, is much resorted to for sea-bathing. The remains of Burlington Church, founded in the reign of Henry I. prove that it must have been a very fine structure. A weekly market is held here, and two annual fairs. Pop. 5037. 20 miles from Scarborough."— Thomson's *New Universal Gazetteer*, Lond., 1837.

"Mr. William Hustler, grandfather to Sir William, was a great benefactor to it. The key which is chiefly frequented by colliers and inhabited by sea-faring people, lies near two miles from the town, which is about 5 furlongs length and gives title of Earl to the noble family of Boyle. Here was formerly a priory."—England's *Gazetteer*, London, 1751.

### Note 5, page 29.

De Vries, in his voyage of 1633, says: "The Bay inside of Sandy Hook is a large one, where fifty to sixty ships can lie, well protected from the winds of the sea. Sandy Hook stretches a full half-mile from the hills, forming a flat, sandy beach, about eight or nine paces wide, and is covered with small blue plum trees, which there grow wild." The same sort of fruit is found there, it is said, at this day.— *Voyages from Holland to America, A. D. 1632 to 1644. By David Pieterson De Vries.* Translated from the Dutch by Mr. Henry C. Murphy, New York, 1853 p. 63, and privately printed by Mr. James Lenox.

De Vries's admirable narrative, and for which, in its English version, all are so much indebted to Mr. Murphy, who has faithfully preserved the spirit of the original, we have never found in fault. The truthfulness, courage, good sense, self reliance and resources of De Vries render the statement of his adventures invaluable to the historical student, a value greatly enhanced from the fact, that he is the only author who speaks of many matters connected with the early history and topography of the Delaware.

*Note 6, page 30.*

See a historical sketch of New Perth in Whitehead's *Contributions to the History of East Jersey.*

*Note 7, page 30.*

The date of the Dutch settlement at *Minesink, Minisincks or Meenesink,* is involved in doubt, and is one of the most interesting problems connected with the history of Pennsylvania. We shall not even venture a conjecture upon the subject. The occupation extended from the beginning of the flats at the northern base of the Blue Mountains, along both sides of the Delaware; and a very interesting account of it may be found in a communication addressed in 1828 to Mr. Samuel Hazard, the editor of the Register, by Samuel Preston, of Stockport, Wayne County, Penna.

In 1787 Preston, who was deputy under John Lukens, surveyor general, received from the latter the facts, which form the subject of this narrative. It appears that the first information of the settlement did not reach the Provincial Government until about 1729, for in that year, it passed a law that all purchases made of the Indians in that region should be void. In 1730 "Nicholas Scull, the famous surveyor, was appointed an agent to investigate the facts," who took with him, as an assistant, John Lukens; and hiring Indian guides, they had a fatiguing journey, there then being no white inhabitants in the upper part of Bucks or Northampton counties, and after great difficulty in leading their horses through the Water Gap to *Meenesink Flats,* they arrived at that place, and found it "all settled with *Hollanders.*" The "remarkable Samuel Depui told them that when the rivers were frozen he had a good road to *Esopus* from the *Mine Holes,* on the *Mine* road, some hundred miles, that he took his wheat and cider there, for salt and necessaries, and did not appear to have any knowledge or idea where the river ran, of the Philadelphia market, or of being in the government of Pennsylvania."

"They were of the opinion that the first settlements of Hollanders, in Meenisink, were many years older than William Penn's charter (in 1681) and as Depui had treated them so well they concluded to make a survey of his claim in order to befriend him if necessary. When they began to survey, the Indians gathered round; and an old Indian laid his hand on N. Scull's shoulder and said '*put up iron string, go home.*' That they quit and returned." This closed the statement of facts as derived from Lukens.

The following is Preston's narrative:

"I had it in charge from John Lukens to learn more particulars respecting the Mine road to Esopus, &c., &c.

"I found Nicholas Depui, Esq. (son of Samuel), living in a spacious stone house, in great plenty and affluence. The old Mine holes were a few miles above on the Jersey side the river, by the lower point of *Paaquarry Flat*, that the Meene-sink settlement extended 40 miles or more, on both sides the river. That he had well known the *Mine road* to *Esopus*, and used, before he opened the boat channel, to drive on it several times every winter with loads of wheat and cider, as also did his neighbors, to purchase their salt and necessaries in Esopus, having then no other market or knowledge where the river ran to: that after a navigable channel was opened, through *Foul Rifts*, they generally took to boating, and most of the settlement turned their trade down stream and the mine road became less and less traveled.

"This interview with the amiable Nicholas Depui, Esq., was in the month of June, 1787; he then appeard to be perhaps about 60 years of age. I interrogated him as to the particulars of what he knew, as to when and by whom the *Mine* road was made, what was the ore they dug and hauled on it, what was the date and from whence or how came the first settlers of *Meene-sink* in such great numbers as to take up all the flats on both sides the river for 40 miles.

"He could only give traditional accounts of what he had heard from older people without date, in substance as follows:

"That in some former age there came a company of miners from *Holland*, supposed from the great labor that had been expended in making that road about 100 miles long, that they were very rich or great people in working the two mines, one on Delaware, where the mountain nearly approaches the lower point of *Paaquarry* flat, the other at the north foot of some mountain near half way between Delaware and Esopus, that he ever understood abundance of ore had been hauled on that road, but never could learn whether it was lead or silver.

"That the first settlers came from Holland to seek a place of quiet, being persecuted for their religion. I believe that they were Arminians, they followed the mine road to the large flats on Delaware, that smoothed cleared land, and such an abundance of large apple trees suited their views, that they bona fide bought the improvements of the native Indians, most of whom then removed to Susquehanna, that with such as remained there was peace and friendship until the year 1755. I then went to view the Paaquarry Mine holes, there appeared to have been a great abundance of labor done there at some former time, but the mouth of these holes were caved full and overgrown with bushes. I concluded to myself if there ever had been a rich mine under that mountain, it must be there yet in close confinement.

"The other old men I conversed with gave their traditions similar to Nicholas Depui, and they all appeared to be the grandsons of the first settlers and generally very illiterate as to dates or anything relating to chronology.

"In the summer of 1789 I began to build on this place, when there came two venerable gentlemen, on a surveying expedition: they were the late General James Clinton, the father of the late De Witt Clinton, and Christopher Tappan, Esq.; he was the clerk and recorder of Ulster county; for many years before they had both been surveyors under General Clinton's father, when he was surveyor general. In order to learn some history from gentlemen of their general knowledge, I accompanied them in the woods; they both well knew the *mine holes*, *mine roads*, and as there were no kind of documents or records thereof, united in opinion, that it was a work transacted while the state of New York belonged to the government of Holland, that it fell to the English in the year 1664, and that the change of government stopped the mining business and that the road must have been made many years before such digging could be done, that it must undoubtedly have been the first good road of any extent ever made in any part of the United States. That from the best evidence that I have been able to obtain, I am clearly of opinion that Meenesink was the oldest European settlement of equal extent ever made in the territory afterwards named Pennsylvania. And these enterprising Arminians and followers of Hugo De Grotius, by their just and pacific conduct to the natives, so as to maintain peace and friendship with them for perhaps one hundred years, have left a traditional memorial of their virtue that time ought not to obliterate."

It seems the best interpretation Scull could make of the word *Meenesink*, was "*the water is gone,*" and Mr. Preston offers the following theory: "From every appearance of so much alluvial or made land, above the mountain, there must, in some former period of the world, have been a great dam against the mountain, that formed all the settlement named Meenesink into

3∙0

a lake, which extended and backed the water at least 50 miles, as appears by the alluvial or made land. What height the dam was, is quite uncertain; had it been as high or half as high as the mountain, the water would have run into the North river, at or near the old mine road or Hudson and Delaware canal. From the water made land, and distance that it appears to have backed over the falls in the river, the height must, at a moderate calculation, have been between 150 and 200 feet — which would have formed a cataract in proportion to the quantity of water similar to Niagara.

"By what convulsion of nature, or in what age of the world, can never be known; but, in my opinion, from every observation that I have been able to make, in so frequently passing through the Gap by water and land, it appears that the dam must have been sunk into some tremendous subterraneous cavern, and to a depth that cannot be known or estimated. * * The distance through the mountain is called two miles, and say, the river will average near half a mile wide, the water as still as a mill pond; so that a raft will float either up or down as the wind blows. As to the depth of the water, I have been told by old men, that formerly they could not find any bottom by sounding with the longest ropes or cords they could obtain.

"Nicholas Scull was esteemed a first rate man of his day as to science and general knowledge. Ninety-eight years ago he was on Depuis' Island, and from the vast size of a hollow buttonwood and apple tree he concluded that the water must have been gone one thousand years or more, for trees to have grown to such an uncommon size." After some further speculations on the subject Mr. Preston naively adds, "if any person thinks my hypothesis erroneous, the *Water Gap will not run away*. They may go and examine for themselves," and we know no spot better deserving scientific explorations.—*Hazard's Register*, 1, 428, 439, 440.

The discrepance between Depuis's alleged ignorance of the existence of Philadelphia or where the river ran, and the statement in the text, will present itself to the reader. We are unable to offer any explanation.

The year 1615 is the alleged date of the settlement of Esopus by the Hollanders (*Answer of Dutch to English Manifesto, Doc. Rel. Col. History of New York*, edited by Dr. O'Callaghan's, II, 325; O'Callaghan's *New Nth.*, 1, 390), and it is probable that the settlers at Meenesink must have found their way there from the former place. Our author does not allude to the existence of copper mines, but so early as 1659 the directors of the Dutch West India Company say "we lately saw a small piece of mineral, said to have been brought from New Netherland, which was such good and pure copper that we deemed it worth enquiry of one Kloos de Ruyter about it, as

we presume he must know, if the fact is as stated." He asserted that there
was a copper mine at Menesink.— *Hazard's Annals*, 255, and *Doc. Rel.
Col. History of New York* II, 633. This was, it is likely, from the mine at
Paaquarry flat, the present *Pahaquarry*, in the northeast corner of War-
ren county, New Jersey. Any discovery of copper must have been made
between the years 1641 and 1649, for, in a *Journal of New Netherland* begun
in the former year (*Doc. Rel. Col. Hist. of N. Y.*, I, 180), it is stated that
in the interior are pretty high mountains, exhibiting generally pretty
strong indications of minerals, and in a document dated 1649 (*Id.*, 262),
fully an hundred different samples of minerals are said to have been
lost on their way to Holland.

In 1715 Governor Hunter of New York, in his letter to the Lords of Trade
referred to a copper mine in New York, "brought to perfection, of which in
one month a ton of ore had been sent to England;" but he does not state
its location—*Doc. Rel. Col. Hist. N. Y.*, V, 462. The same authority states
that in 1720 "there was iron enough, that copper was rarer. lead at a great
distance in the Indian settlement, and coal mines on *Long Island*, but not yet
wrought," and in 1721 "a great quantity of iron ore was stated to exist in
New Jersey, and some copper."—*Id.*, 556, 603.

### *Note 8, page 31.*

Our knowledge of the first attempt at establishing a whale fishery upon the Delaware is derived from the account contained in the narrative of
that most minute, truthful and graphic of all voyagers, David Pietersz. de
Vries, to which we have before referred. This navigator, with whom was
associated eight others, formed themselves into a patroonship, and "at the
same time equipped a ship with a yacht for the purpose of prosecuting the
voyage, as well as to carry on the whale fishery in that region, as to plant
a colony for the cultivation of all sorts of grain, for which the country is
very well adapted, and of tobacco. This ship, with the yacht, sailed from
the Texel, the 12th of December, 1630, with a number of people and a
large stock of cattle, to settle our colony upon the South river,[1] which
lies on the 38th and half degree, and to conduct the whale fishery there, as
Godyn represented that there were many whales which kept before
the bay, and the oil at sixty guilders a hogshead he thought would
realize a good profit, and consequently that fine country be cultivated."
This attempt was unsuccessful; the captain on his return to Holland reporting that they had arrived too late in the season for their purpose. "It was
therefor again resolved to undertake a voyage for the whale fishery, and
that I myself (De Vries) should go as patroon, and as commander of the
ship and yacht and should endeavor to be there in December, in order to

[1] The Delaware.

conduct the whale fishery during the winter, as the whales come in the winter and remain till March." De Vries accordingly sailed and found, on his arrival at Swanendael, that the little colony had been murdered by the Indians; not a soul was left to tell the tale, and its particulars and the cause which led to the sad event were ascertained from the natives themselves. Our navigator allowed his people to prosecute their undertaking at Swanendael, while he sailed up the river. On his return he found seven whales had been caught, "but there were only thirty-two cartels of oil obtained, so that the whale fishery is very expensive when such meagro fish are caught. We could have done more if we had had good harpooners, for they had struck seventeen fish and only secured seven, which was astonishing. They had always struck the whales in the tail. I afterwards understood from some Basques, who were old whale fishers, that they always struck the harpoon in the fore part of the back. This voyage was an expensive one to us, but not so much, since I had laid in a good cargo of salt in the West Indies, which brought a good price. Having put our oil in the ship, taken down our kettle and hauled in wood and water, we got ready to sail."—*De Vries's Voyages*, translated by Mr. Henry C. Murphy, and privately printed by Mr. James Lenox, New York, 1853.— This appears to be the most circumstantial narrative extant of any attempt to prosecute whale fishing, as a commercial enterprise. The trade seems to have continued of some importance, and so late as 1693 was made the subject of an enactment, for in that year a law was passed, in which a preamble set forth that, Whereas, the *whalery* in Delaware Bay has been in so great a measure invaded by strangers and foreigners, that the greatest part of Oyl and Bone recovered and got by that imploy, hath been exported out of the Province to the great detriment thereof, to obviate which mischief *Be it enacted*, &c., that all Persons not residing within the Precincts of this Province, or the Province of Pennsylvania, who shall kill, or bring on shore any whale or whales within Delaware Bay or elsewhere within the Boundaries of this Government shall pay one full entire Tenth of all the Oyl and Bone, made out of the said Whale or Whales unto the present Government of the Province for the Time being.—*Leaming and Spicer*, 519 and 520, Chapter ix of Laws of the Province of West New Jersey.

### *Note 9, page 35.*

The cultivation of the grape, especially with reference to the production of wine, very early attracted the attention of the emigrants to America, of which fact some remarkable evidence is upon record. And it is curious to compare the sanguine expectations upon this subject, and upon the raising of silk, with the results of two hundred and fifty years' experience.

Our progenitors, mostly coming from a land where the sun was oftener clouded than unobscured, warmed into enthusiasm under the genial influences of a more southern sky. Their spirits were led captive, and their descriptions, imbued with the language of poetry, held forth to the fortunate adventurer all the good the most fruitful imagination could conceive of what the earth might produce or the air and water contained for the comfort and advantage of the race.

In a curious tract entitled A DECLARATION OF THE STATE OF *the* COLONIE and Affaires in VIRGINIA: WITH the Names of the Adventurors, and Summes adventured in that Action. By his Majesties Counseil for VIRGINIA, 22 Iunij, 1620. LONDON: Printed by T. S., 1620, 8vo, pp. 30 and 39, the advantages are set forth in terms sufficient to allure the most unimaginative aspirant for better fortune. "And first to remove that unworthy aspersion, wherewith ill-disposed mindes, guiding their Actions by corrupt ends, have, both by Letters from thence, and by rumours here at home, sought unjustly to staine and blemish that Countrey, as being barren and unprofitable :— Wee have thought it necessary, for the full satisfaction of all, to make it publikely knowne, that, by diligent examination, wee have assuredly found, those Letters and Rumours to have been false and malicious ; procured by practise, and suborned to evill purposes, and contrarily disadvowed by the testimony, upon Oath, of the chiefe Inhabitants of all the Colony ; by whom we are ascertained, that the countrey is rich, spacious, and well watered ; temperate as for the climate ; very healthfull after men are a little accustomed to it : abounding with all God's naturall blessings : The Land replenished with the goodliest Woods in the world, and those full of *Deere*, and other Beasts for sustenance : The Seas and Rivers (whereof many are exceeding faire and navigable) full of excellen tFish, and of all Sorts desireable ; both Water and Land yeelding Fowle in very great store and variety ; In Summe, a Countrey, too good for ill people : and wee hope reserved by the providence of God, for such as shall apply themselves faithfully to his service, and be a strength and honour to our King and Nation. But touching those Commodities for which that Countrey is proper, and which have beene lately set up for the adventurors benefit : wee referre you to a true note of them latety delivered in a great and generall Court, and hereunto annexed for your better information * * * The riche Furres, Caviary and Cordage, which we draw from Russia with so great difficulty, are to be had in *Virginia*, and the parts adjoyning, with case and plenty. The Masts, Planckes and Boords, the Pitch and Tarre, the Pot-ashes and Sope-ashes, the Hempe and Flax ( being the materials of Linnen), which now wee fetch from *Norway, Denmarke, Poland*, and *Germany*, are there to be had in abundance and great perfection. The *Iron* which hath so wasted our

*English* Woods, that itself in short time must decay together with them, is to be had in *Virginia* (where wasting of woods is a benefit) for all good conditions answerable to the best in the world. The Wines, Fruits, and Salt of *France* and *Spaine :* The silkes of *Persia* and *Italie*, will be found also in Virginia, and in no Kinde of worth inferior: Wee omit here a multitude of other naturall commodities, dispersed up and downe the divers parts of the world : of Woods, Rootes and Berries, for excellent Dyes : of Plants and all other Druggs, for Physicall service : of sweet Woods, Oyles, and Gummes, for pleasure and other use : of Cotten-Wooll and Sugar-Canes : all which may there also be had in abundance, with an infinity of other more : And will conclude with these three ; Corne, Cattle, and Fish, which are the substance of the foode of man. The Graines of our Countrey doe prosper there very well : of Wheate they have great plenty : But their *Maze* being the naturall Graine of that Countrey, doth farre exceede in pleasantnesse, strength and fertility. The Cattle which we have transported thither (being now growne neere to five hundred), become much bigger of Body, than the breed from which they came : The Horses also more beautifull and fuller of courage. And such is the extraordinary fertility of that Soyle, that the *Does* of their *Deere* yeelde two Fawnes at a birth, and sometimes three. The Fishings at *Cape Codd*, being within those Limits, will in plenty of Fish be equall to those of *Newfound Land*, and in goodnesse, and greatnesse, much superiour. To conclude, it is a Countrey, which nothing but ignorance can thinke ill of, and which no man, but of, a corrupt minde and ill purpose can defame."

The importance attached to the production of wine was discussed in a subsequent tract entitled " VIRGINIA : More especially the south part thereof Richly and truly valued, viz : The fertile *Carolana*, and no lesse excellent Isle of *Roanoak*, of Latitude from 31. to 37. Degr. relating the meanes of raysing infinite profits to the Adventurers, and Planters. The second Edition, with Addition of THE DISCOVERY OF SILKWORMS, with their benefit, And Implanting of Mulberry Trees. ALSO the Dressing of Vines, for the rich Trade of making Wines in VIRGINIA, Together with the making of the Saw-mill, &c., &c. By E. W. Gent," London, 1650, pp. 56, 8vo.

The author signs himself in his preface Ed Williams, but we have not been able to ascertain the date of publication of his first edition, he says "That wild Vines runne naturally over *Virginia*, occular experience declares who delighting in the Neighbourhood of their beloved Mulbery-trees inseparable associates over all that countrey, and of which in this their wildnesse, Wines have been made, of these vines if transplanted and cultivated, there can be made no doubt but a Rich and Generous Wine would be produced ; But if wee set the Greeke, Cyprian, Candian or Calabrian

12

Grape, those Countries lying parallel with this, there neede not be made the smallest question, but it would be a staple, which would enrich this Countrey to the envy of France and Spaine, and furnish the Northerne parts of Europe, and China itself, where they plant it not (of which more heereafter), with the Noblest Wine in the World, at no excessive prices. * * * For the advance of which noble staple, I should propose that the Greeke, and other Rich Vines, being procured from the Countries, to which they are genial, every Planter in that Country might be enjoyned to keep a constant Nursery, to the end when the ground is cleared that they may be fit for removal and the Vineyard speedily planted.

"Further, that some Greek and other Viguevons might be hired out of these Countries to instruct us in the labour, and lest their envy, pride, or jealousie of being layd aside when their mysterie is discovered may make them too reserved in communicating their knowledge, they may be assured, besides the continuance of their Pension of a share of the profits of every mans Vintage. * * That before their going over a general consultation may be had whith them, what ground is proper, what season fit, what prevention of casualties by bleeding or splitting, what way to preserve or restore Wine when vesseld, which *species* of Wine is fittest for transportation over, or retention in the Countrey, which for duration, which for present spending: It being in experience manifest that some Wines refine themselves by purge upon the sea, others by the same meanes suffer an evaporation of their Spirits, joyne to this that some Wines collect strength and richnesse, others contract feetlenesse and sowernesse by seniority," pp. 6, 8.

Our author closes his delineation in these quaint sentences, and highly colored as they must, to his unimaginative countrymen, have seemed, the lapse of two centuries and a half does not falsify his predictions. The "opulence" he describes exists; the "Eden," of his beloved Virginia may not have been realized, but the future has great good in store when the clouds which now envelop her shall have passed away.

"The incomparable Virgin hath raised her dejected head, cleared her enclouded reputation, and now like the Eldest Daughter of Nature expresseth a priority in her Dowry; her browes encircled with opulency to be believed by no other triall, but that of experience, her unwounded wombe has of all those Treasuries which indeere Provinces to respect of glory, and may with as great justice as any Countrey the Sunne honours with his eye-beames, entitle herself to an affinity with Eden, to an absolute perfection above all but Paradize.

"And this those Gentlemen to whom she vouchsafes the honour of her Embrees, when by the blessings of God upon their labours sated with the beauty of their Cornefield, they shall retire into their Groves checkered with

Vines, Olives, Mirtles, from thence dilate themselves into their Walkes covered in a manner, paved with Oranges and Lemmons, whence surfeited with variety, they incline to repose in their Gardens upon nothing less perfumed then Roses and Gilly-flowers. When they shall see their numerous Heards wanton with the luxury of their Pasture, confesse a narrownesse in their Barnes to receive their Corne, in bosomes to expresse fully their thankefulness to the Almighty Author of these blessings, will chearefully confesse: Whilst the Incomparable Roanoake like a Queene of the Ocean, encircled with an hundred attendant Islands and the most Majestick Carolana shall in such an ample and noble gratitude by her improvement repay her Adventurers and Creditors with an Interest so far transcending the Principal," pp. 44, 45.

The grape grew indigenously in Pennsylvania and New Jersey and attracted the attention not of the early navigators only, but of the first settlers, and in their descriptions of the country, is frequently spoken of by both. It was found in great abundance along the shores of the Delaware, and De Vries in the account of his voyage of 1633, p. 40, appears to have been the first who mentions it, remarking, "this is a fine country in which many vines grow wild, so that we gave it the name of *Wyngærts kill*." The creek to which he refers may have been the present Oldmans creek in New Jersey, or he may have intended to indicate the region between Naamans creek and Wilmington, Delaware. Lindstrom, the Swedish engineer, in his MS. map of the Delaware (of 1651), entitles the point of land immediately south of Oldmans creek, "*Drufwe udden, Le Cap des Raisins*," and the country below Naamans creek, on the opposite shore, "*Windrufwe udden, Le Cap des Raisins*." Penn had great expectaions from the cultivation of the grape, and frequently mentions it, with reference to the production of wine, as do others who came with or followed him—expectations which have not as yet been to any extent realized.

### Note 10, page 37.

"Mum; a malt liquor, which derives its name from the inventor, *Mumme*, a German. It was formerly exported from Germany in large quantities, but is now less used." — *Encyclopædia Americana*.

Andrew Yarranton, in his work entitled *England's Improvements by Sea and Land*, recommends its manufacture and says:

"*Stratford* upon *Avon*, in *Warwickshire*, will be a very good place to build Granaries to receive Corn; * * * There may as much Mum be made there, as at present is made at Brunswick: And there Mum may be made and sent into Ireland, West-Indies, France, Spain, and into the Mediterranean; And these Granaries will be the occasion of getting away the Mum-Trade from Brunswick; This shews as like a *Romance* as doth the Title-page of my Book, unless I do give you reasons for what I say, and shew you how it may be brought to pass, the which I will do: Observe, the Mum at Brunswick is made of Wheat, and the Wheat that it is made of, is brought from the Granaries at *Magdenbury* and *Shenibank*, and it grows in the vale of *Parinburg;* when it comes to Brunswick it is malted, and so made into Mum; and when made. then sent by Land to the river *Elb,* and so to *Hamborough:* and from thence disposed by Merchants unto all Parts: But the Mum at Brunswick is a Medicine, and drinks very nauseous, and is not there drinkable at all: but that which makes it good palitable and strong is its being long at sea; There it is forc'd into a fermentation, and that keeps it working, whereby it alters the very property of the liquor; and were it not to be sent to sea, that trade at *Brunswick* would not be worth anything; and to convince you further of the reason of what I say. take this one thing, and that will confirm you in the truth of the rest. Our *English* Beer Brewed at *London*, and carried to sea, and landed at *Hamborough*, and so carried up the *Elb* as far as *Draisden*. the Duke of *Saxonies'* Court, and in those Parts, it is sold for six pence a quart; and it is not like the Beer either for Tast, Strength, or Pleasantness, as it was when here; the Sea having put it into a fermentation causeth it to drink pleasant strong and delightful, even comparable to *March-Beer* in England four Years old, which is well-brewed and grown very mellow." p. 118.

An inquiry which a friend,[1] in behalf of the editor, took the pains to insert in the London *Notes and Queries*, has elicited some curious information on this topic:

"In Playford's *Second Book of the Musical Companion*, N. Pearson, 1715, is the following *Catch in Praise of Mum:*

| | |
|---|---|
| There's an odd sort of liquor | And as strong as six horses, |
| New come from Hamborough, | Coach and all, |
| 'Twill stick a whole wapentak | As I told you 'twill make you |
| Thorough and thorough; | As drunk as a drum: |
| 'Tis yellow, and likewise | You'd fain know the name on't? |
| As bitter as gall, | But for that, my friend, mum. |

In a curious little book — *Political Merriment*, or *Truths to Set to Some Tune*, 1714 — is a short poem "In Praise of Brunswick Mum" (p. 96), and at page 3, same work, "An Excellent Ballad," concluding with a stanza relating to mum. Pope also says, somewhere,

The clamorous crowd is hush'd with mugs of *mum*,
Till all, tun'd equal, sound a general hum."

*N. and Q.*, 3d s., vii, p. 41.

1 Mr. Thomas Stewardson Jr., of Philadelphia, to whose friendly aid we are indebted for further information.

*Mum.* "It may be worth recording that the word *mum* is at least as old as the beginning of the 16th century. In the treatise De Generibus Elnosorum et Ebrietate Vitanda, written A.D. 1515, occurs a chapter on the various kinds of beer then in use in Germany. Among a host of other names occurs that of *Mommon sive Mommun Brunsvigeii.*"

JOHN ELIOT HODGKIN,<br>From *Notes and Queries*, 3d s., vii, 163.

"Barclay, in his *Dictionary*, states this to be a strong liquor, brought from Brunswick or Germany. Ash defines it 'beer brewed from wheat.' I have, however, a curious old dictionary in 18mo, no name, but about 1700, which says: '*Mum*, a kind of physical beer, made (originally) at Brunswick or Germany with *husks* of Walnut infused.' Is this correct? If so, is the manufacture carried on there now? Or is there any record of Walnuts being used in brewing? And again, is the green shell, or what part of the fruit used? Broom tops formerly were employed in England for giving a bitter to beer, and are so to the present day in Italy. Many sorts of bitter have also been tried. This is the first, however, I have heard of Walnut in any form."

A. A., *Poet's Corner.*

The following is from a manuscript note book in my possession, bearing date 1738:

"Mum is a sort of sweet malt liq'r, brewed with barley and hops and a small mixture of wheat; very thick, scarce drinkable till purified at Sea. It is transported into other countries. Hides and Mum chief trade of Brunswick, Wolfenbottel."

W. TISHWICK,<br>*Notes and Queries*, 3d series, viii, 100.

### Note 11, page 39.

Considerable attention was paid, at an early period, to the breed of horses in the colonies. The founder of Pennsylvania was very fond of the propagation of good stock, and, according to Mr. Dixon, "the love of fine horses, which the Englishman shares with the Arab, did not forsake him in the New World. At his first visit to America, he carried over three blood mares, a fine white horse, not of full breed, and other inferior animals, not for breeding but for labor. His inquiries about the mares were as frequent and minute as those about the gardens; and when he went out for the second time, in 1699, he took with him the magnificent colt, Tamerlane, by the celebrated Godolphin Barb, to which the best horses in England trace their pedigree."—Dixon's *Penn., Amer. ed., p. 207.

In a letter by Penn, addressed from Philadelphia in 1683 to The Com-

*mittee of the Free Society of Traders, Residing in London*, he says: "We have no want of horses, and some are very 'good and shapely enough; two ships have been freighted to Barbadoes, with horses and pipe staves, since my coming in."

The breed of horses in New England, at least so far as related to Massachusetts, appears, prior to 1688, to have deteriorated; for in that year a stringent law was passed, for the purpose of correcting the evil. And in Connecticut, as well as in Rhode Island, much care was given to the rearing of good stock.—Palfrey's *Hist. of New England*, iii, p. 54, in note.

*Note 12, page 39.*

Our author here refers to the iron works of Col. Morris, which were in Monmouth county.—*Morris Papers*, p. 3; Whitehead's *East Jersey*, 271. These were the first works in New Jersey, as those at Durham, below Easton, near the Delaware, were the first in Pennsylvania.

The earliest allusion to the existence of iron that we have been able to discover may be found in a tract, entitled "A TRUE DECLARATION OF THE ESTATE OF THE COLONIE IN VIRGINIA, with a confutation of severall scandalous reports as have tended to the disgrace of so worthy an enterprise, Published by advice and direction of the Councell of Virginia," London, 1610. Sir Thomas Gates represented that "there are divers sorts of Minueralls especially of Iron oare, lying upon the ground for ten miles circuite, of which we have made triall at home that it makes as good iron as any in Europe."

In a subsequent and rare tract, probably by Sir Edwin Sandys, styled A DECLARATION OF THE STATE *of the* COLONIE *and Affaires in* VIRGINIA, &c., London, 1620, and to which allusion has been made. The writer states that in 1619, there were sent to that colony "out of *Warwickshire* and *Staffordshire* about one hundred and ten: and out of *Sussex* about forty; all framed to *Iron*-workes." Among the "commodities" to which "these people are directed principally to apply, next to their own necessary maintenance," he enumerates "*Iron:* for which are sent 150 Persons, to set up three *Iron* workes; proofe having been made of the extraordinary goodness of that *Iron.*" What success attended this adventure we have not been able to discover. Williams, in his tract entitled "*Virginia*," &c., London, 1650, and to which a more particular reference is made in a note, says: "But that in which there will be an extraordinary use of our Woods is the Iron mills, which if once erected, will be an undecaying staple, and of this forty servants will by their labour raise to the Adventurer foure thousand pound yearely: Which may easily be apprehended, if wee consider the deereness of Wood in England, where notwithstanding this great clog of difficulty, the Master of the Mill gaines so much yearely, that he cannot but reckon himselfe a provident Saver.  Neither does Virginia yeeld, to any other Province whatsoever, in excellency and plenty of this oare: And I cannot promise to myselfe any other then extraordinary successe and gaine, if this noble and usefull Staple be but vigorously followed.

"And indeed it had long ere this growne to a full perfection, if the treachery of the Indians had not crushed it in the beginning, and the backwardnesse of the *Virginia* Merchants to reerect it, hindred that countrey from the benefit arising from that universall staple."

In an appendix is to be found "A Valuation of the Commodities growing and to be had in Virginia: valued in the year 1621," where iron is set down at "*Ten pounds the Tun.*"  We think this may be accepted in proof that the colonists of 1619 had succeeded in smelting iron ore, but that the production had been hindered by the causes mentioned by Williams.  The tract published in 1650 was a second edition: and if merely a republication of the first edition, we have no means of assigning a date to the facts which he relates.  It is, however, we think, to be presumed that if any fresh attempts had been made towards the establishment of works the author would have mentioned the circumstance.

The Dutch government were, it appears, at a very early period, alive to the value of the discovery of minerals; for in 1646, Hudde received directions from William Kieft, director general of the New Netherlands, "to inquire about certain minerals in this country."  "For this purpose, he went to Sankikans and tried to penetrate to the great falls, where, if the samples might be credited, there was a great hope of success, when," says Hudde, "I would pass the first fall,[1] a sachem, named Wirakeken, stopped me, and asked where I would go.  I answered I intended to go upward.  He replied I was not permitted, and asked what is my object.  He at last informed me that the Swedish governor told one Meerkedt, a sachem residing near Tinnekonk, that we intended to build a house near the great falls, and that in the vessels which we expected near 250 men would arrive to be sent from the Manhattans, who would kill all the savages below on the river, and that this fort was to be garrisoned in the house which we intended to build, and would prevent the savages residing up the river to come to their assistance, so that no more would be able to escape; and in proof of all this, that we would first come up in a small vessel to visit and explore the spot, and that we would kill two savages as a pretext, but that Printz would never permit it, and would certainly expel us from the river."  All attempts to go up to the falls being ineffectual, as he was stopped every time, the project was necessarily abandoned by

[1] At Trenton, N. J.

Hudde."—Hazard's *Annals of Penn.*, 87. Thus, owing to the watchful jealousy of the Swedish governor Printz, in exciting the fears of the Indians, the discovery of iron and other ore was delayed. It is probable the region to which Hudde desired to penetrate was either the Meenesink, and where in all likelihood a Dutch colony already existed, or it may have been the country in the neighborhood of Durham, in Bucks county, Pennsylvania, where the earliest attempt at the manufacture of iron was made.

Campanius, the Swedish historian, of what afterwards constituted the States of Pennsylvania, Delaware and New Jersey (Stockholm, 1702), and whose work was translated by Mr. Du Ponceau, and published by the Historical Society of Pennsylvania, although minutely describing the productions of the country, does not allude to the existence of iron. And it is equally curious that Penn, in his letter of 1683 to the Society of Free Traders, and which was the result of close personal observation, says nothing of iron, although his object is evidently to impart information for the benefit and encouragement of emigrants.—See Letter in Proud's *Penn.*, I, 246, In a description of Pennsylvania entitled "*Some Accounts of the Province,*" and published by him previously to his embarkation (London, 1681), he speaks of iron among the "commodities" "that the country is *thought* to be capable of."—*Hazard's Register.* I, 307.

The earlier statistics upon the subject of iron are very meagre. Mr. French has attempted to collect them and states that the pig and bar iron exported to Great Britain by the American Colonies from 1728 to 1748, and from 1750 to 1755, inclusive, "amounted to 58,000 tons," and upon separating the items we find the remarkable fact that during these years the total amount exported from Pennsylvania was 8,012 tons against 48,912 from Maryland and Virginia.—*History of Rise and Progress of the Iron Trade in the United States,* &c. By B. F. French, 1858.

The mother country was jealous of her colonies, and when competition was found likely to interfere with home production, an act of Parliament was passed to crush the incipient spirit of enterprise. It was as to iron, however, discovered that it would be promotive of home interests to allow the creation of the raw material, in the form of pigs and bars, but not its further manufacture, so it was enacted that the importation of pig and bar iron should be encouraged, but that the "erection of any Mill or other Engine for slitting or rolling of iron, or any plating Forge to work with a Tilt Hammer, or any Furnace for making steel should not be permitted," and the respective Governors were required to return a list of such as were erected prior to the 24th of January 1750. We consequently find that William Branson and Stephen Paschall were returned as the owners of a Furnace [1]

1 At the N. W. corner of Walnut and 8th streets, built in 1747, Philadelphia.

in Philadelphia, for making steel, and John Hall as the owner of a Plating Forge with Tilt Hammer in Biberry Township, Philadelphia county, both erected, however, prior to 1750. No such works were returned as existing in Bucks or Lancaster counties and that "one such Mill" had been erected in 1746 by John Taylor, in Thornbury Township, Chester county, *Colonial Records*, V, 458; *Id.*, IX, 632; *Pensylvania Archives*, II, 52.

The lapse of one hundred years made a great change in the productive capacity of the iron works of Pennsylvania, for in 1850 we find her in possession of 504 establishments; of these 64 were Anthracite Blast Furnaces, 230 Charcoal Hot and Cold Blast, 4 Coke and Hot Blast, 6 Bloomeries, 121 Forges, 79 Rolling Mills. Of the Furnaces five were unfinished, and of the rest, owing to the depressed state of the manufacture, more than half were out of blast. Of the 62 counties then constituting the state 45 possessed iron works. The amount of capital invested was $20,502,076, of which $1,837,000 belonged to capitalists in Alleghany county.

The actual make in 1849 in Pennsylvania by Furnaces of all
descriptions, was ........................................................ 253,035 tons
By Forges............................................................... 29,240 "
" Rolling Mills.................................................... 108,358 "

For which facts we are indebted to a valuable work entitled "Documents relating to the Manufacture of Iron in Pennsylvania," &c. By Mr. Charles E. Smith, Philadelphia, 1850.

The total manufacture in 1849, and in Pennsylvania itself amounted to 390,633 tons, exceeding, so far as imperfect statistics enable us to judge, by more than six times the total production of the whole country beginning with the year 1728 and ending with 1755, exclusive of the year 1740, of which we have no account.

In 1859, probably owing to the reverses in the trade, the number of iron works in Pennsylvania were but 410: In New Jersey there were 80, in Maryland 34 and in Virginia, which at one time stood preëminent in the manufacture, but 82.

### Note 13, page 40.

According to the " *Declaration of the State of the Colonie and Affaires of Virginia*, &c.," London, 1620, p. 4, already quoted, the *cotton plant* appears to have been indigenous to that colony.

In Williams's *Virginia*, London, 1650, also cited, "*cotton wool*, at 8*d.* the pound," is named in the "Valuation of the Commodities growing and to be had in Virginia: valued in the year 1621." "And since those times improved in all more or lesse," &c.

### Note 14, page 42.

In a work by Ed. Williams, entitled Virginia's *Discovery of* Silke Wormes, with their benefit, &c., Together with the making of the Saw-mill, very usefull in *Virginia* for cutting of Timber, &c., pp. 78, London. 1650, is a representation of a saw-mill, in which, from casual observation, very little, if any difference, can be observed from the mill of the present day.

The author, at the close of his tract, remarks: "This Engine is very common in Norway and Mountaines of Sweden, wherewith they cut great quantity of Deal-bords; which Engine is very necessary to be in a great Towne or Forrest, to cut Timber, whether into planks or otherwise.

This heer[1] is not altogether like those of Norway; for they make the piece of Timber approch the Sawes on certaine wheels with teeth; but because of reparations which those toothd wheeles are often subject unto, I will omit that use: and in stead thereof, put two weights, about 2 or 300 pound weight apiece, whereof one is marked A the other B. The Cords wherewith the sayd weights doe hang. to be fastned at the end of the 2 peeces of moving wood, which slide on two other peeces of fixed wood, by the means of certaine small pulleys, which should be within the house, and so the sayd weights should alwayes draw the sayd peeces of moving wood, which advancing alwayes towards the Sawes rising and falling, shall quickly be cut into 4. 5. or 6. peeces, as you shall, pleas put on Saws, and placed at what distance you will have for the thickness of the planks or bords ye will cut: and when a peece is cut, then let one with a Lever turne a Rowler, whereto shall be fastned a strong Cord which shall bring backe the sayd peece of wood, and lift again the weights: and after put aside the peece already cut, to take againe the Sawes against another peece of wood. Which once done the ingenious Artist may easily convert the same to an Instrument of threshing wheat, breaking of hempe or flax, and other as profitable uses."

### Note 15. Page 43.

The first legislation upon the subject of education, on this continent was attempted by the Virginia Company, in the establishment of a *College* for the training of Indian children, and for this purpose land was granted for its support and in 1619 and 1620 fifty "men were sent, by their labours to bear up the charge of bringing up thirty of the *Infidels* children, in true Religion and civility" and one hundred "tenants for the Colleges Land."

The management of the *College* was by the CXXV chapter of the *Orders and Constitutions ordained by the Treasuror* Counseil and *Companie of Virginia* placed in the hands of a committee who were appointed by the Quarter

---

[1] Referring to the representation.

Court, for a year, and were required "to take into their care the matter of the College to be erected for the conversion of Infidels."—*A Declaration of the state of the Colonie in Virginia*, 6, 3, 36.

In the *Great Charter of Liberties*, as it was styled by the people, or *Frame* of Government, as it was designated by Penn, and which, as its preamble sets out, was "contrived, and composed to the great end of all government, viz. to support power in reverence with the people, and to secure the people from the abuse of power; that they may be free by their just obedience and the magistrates, honorable for their just administration, for liberty without obedience in confusion and obedience without liberty is slavery" it was provided "that the Governor and Provincial council shall erect and order all public schools and reward the authors of useful sciences and laudable inventions in the said province."

At a council held at Philadelphia the 26th 10th month (December), 1683, and at which Penn was present, this power seems to have been for the first time exercised, and the following entry which portrays the simplicity of the times, and the solicitude of the government upon the subject, may be found not uninteresting.

"The Govr and Provincial Council, having taken into their Serious Consideration the great Necessity there is, of a Scool Master for the Instruction and Sober Education of Youth in the Towne of Philadelphia, Sent for Enock flower, an Inhabitant of the said Towne, who for twenty year past hath been excercised, in that care, and Imployment in England, to whom, having Communicated their Minds, he Embraced it upon these following Termes : to Learne to read English 4, s. by the Quarter, to Learne to read and write 6, s. by ye Quarter, to Learne to read, Write and Cast accot 8, s. by ye Quarter; for Boarding a Scholler, that is to say dyet, Washing, Lodging and Scooling, Tenn pounds for one whole year."—*Colonial Records*, I, p. 91.

In the following month it was proposed, in the council "That care be taken about the Learning and Instruction of Youth to Witt: a scool of Arts and Siences." This proposition does not appear to have been carried out but the suggestion is remarkable as presenting the earliest indication in the history of the Province, of an attempt to secure advantages upon a scale more extended, than those afforded by instruction in the simpler branches of education. The Friends Public School which was established in 1689, had its origin perhaps, in this expression of the opinion of the Council. This noted Institution, which to this day in Philadelphia, flourishes in full vigor, was incorporated in 1697, and its charter was confirmed by a fresh Patent from Penn in 1701 and by another in 1708, whereby the corporation was " For ever there after to consist of fifteen discreet and religious persons, of the people called Quakers, by the name of the over seers of the Public School, founded in Philadelphia, at the request, cost, and charges, of the people called Quakers:" Its last charter, confirming all the preceeding and enlarging the powers of the corporation was conferred in 1711.

The benefits were not restricted to the Society, and Robert Proud the Historian of the State, and who at a subsequent period was the head Master thus speaks of it : "This was the first Institution of the kind, in Pennsylvania, intended not only to facilitate the acquisition of the more generally used parts of learning, among all ranks, or degrees, of the people (the poorer sort being taught gratis, and the rich or more wealthy, still paying a proportion for their childrens' instruction) but also the better, and more extensively to promote a virtuous and learned education, than could be effected by any other manner, was the end of the design ; which to the preamble in the said present charter, is thus expressed, viz :

" Whereas, the prosperity and welfare of any people depend in great measure, upon the good education of youth, and their early introduction in the principles of true religion and virtue, and qualifying them to serve their country and themselves by breeding them in reading, writing, and learning of languages, and useful arts and sciences, suitable to their sex age and degree ; which cannot be effected in any manner so well as by erecting *public schools*, for the purposes aforesaid," &c.

" For these laudable purposes, therefore, a number of the principal inhabitants of Philadelphia, being Quakers, in the Fifth month the year (1689), agreed with George Keith, who then resided at Freehold, now called Monmouth, in New Jersey, to undertake the charge. He accordingly removed to Philadelphia, and was the first master of that school ; but continued only about one year".—Proud's *History of Penn.*, I, 343.

Keith who afterwards became famous in the controversial history of the Province was succeeded by his usher Thomas Makin.

Makin was afterward clerk of the assembly, but is better known as the author of a Latin poem "*Descriptio Pennsylvaniæ*, Anno, 1729." In the following lines he alludes to his connection with the grammar school.

> "Hic in gymnasiis linguæ docentum et artes
> Ingenuæ: hic multis doctor et ipse fui.
> Una schola hic alias etiam supereminet omnes,
> *Romano et Græco* quæ docet ore loqui."

Which Proud renders,

> "Here schools for learning, and for arts are seen,
> In which to many I've a teacher been :
> But one, in teaching, doth the rest excel,
> To know and speak the Greek and Latin well."—*Proud*, ii, 370.

The provision on the subject of public schools incorporated in the first and the succeeding frames of government of the province again found a place in the constitution of 1776.

"A school or schools shall be established in each county, by the Legislature, for the convenient instruction of youth, with such salaries to the masters paid, by the Public, as may enable them to instruct youth at low prices : And all useful learning shall be duly encouraged and promoted in one or more universities." Sec. 44, ch. ii.

At the period of the adoption of this constitutional enactment but one college existed in the province. The academy established in 1749 through the agency of a few public spirited individuals among whom was Dr. Franklin, was incorporated in 1753. In 1755 a college was grafted upon it, and in 1779 the property of the institutions was vested, by an act of assembly in trustees, and the "University of the State of Pennsylvania" was created. Academies now began to multiply and were incorporated, and to some extent endowed by the state. Dickinson and Franklin Colleges were incorporated.

In 1770 a new constitution was established in which was this direction.

"Article vii, sect. i. The Legislature shall, as soon as conviently may be, provide by law, for the establishment of schools throughout the state, in such manner that the poor may be taught gratis.

"Sect. ii. The arts and sciences shall be promoted in one or more seminaries of learning."

This requirement of the constitution was disregarded for twelve years, when, on the first of March, 1802, an act of assembly was passed, by which the guardians and overseers of the poor in the city of Philadelphia, of the district of the Northern Liberties, and of every township and borough throughout the commonwealth, were directed to ascertain the names of all those children whose parents or guardians were judged to be unable to provide an education, and to subscribe at the usual rates, and send such children to any neighboring school. This act expired in 1805, but was in terms reënacted in 1809.

It was almost immediately from necessity, an unpopular statute, and although in some instances obeyed, it was in many abused.

In 1818 the city and county of Philadelphia was erected into the first school district; and the first general act which appears to have been of any benefit was passed in the same year. The foundation of our present system of common schools in Pennsylvania was laid in 1824.

Eleven years afterwards (in 1835), the number of schools in Pennsylvania was 762; of teachers, 808; and the average number of scholars in

attendance was 32,544. By the report of the superintendent for the year
ending first June, 1864, the number of schools had increased to 12,930; of
teachers to 15,907; of scholars to 471,267; and the amount expended in
the state, exclusive of Philadelphia, was over two millions of dollars.

The annual message of Mr. Alexander Henry, mayor of Philadelphia,
to the councils, presented in April, 1865, states that the amount expended
in that city during the year 1864, by the board of controllers was $875,889;
and that the number of pupils, irrespective of 3,297, "whose admission
was denied for want of accommodation," was 71,838, exceeding in the city
alone, according to the best computation, by 22,000, the entire amount
of taxables in the province one hundred years ago.

## PUBLIC SCHOOLS IN NEW JERSEY.

We are indebted for the following interesting sketch of the origin of the
system of public instruction in New Jersey to the valuable report of Mr.
F. W. Record, state superintendent, made to the legislature of that state
in the year 1863.

"There was a period in the history of our commonwealth when the
governor, council and deputies in general assembly arrived, for the first
time, at the conclusion that 'the cultivating of learning and good manners
tends greatly to the good and benefit of mankind;' and, under the impression that it was a part of their business to do some little ' good and benefit'
for mankind, they passed an act, entitled ' An act to establish Schoolmasters within this Province.' This was actually making a beginning, and a
very good beginning too, and, perhaps, it was all that was necessary at
the time; but no sooner had the work of establishing schoolmasters fairly
commenced, than it was found necessary to do something more than make
a mere beginning. It became apparent, within three years, that the 'cultivating of learning and good manners' was destined to be a flourishing
business, and that the general assembly must do something more than
'establish Schoolmasters.' Accordingly, we now find them discussing the
propriety of appointing men in the different townships to look after the
schoolmasters, and to make good bargains with them, and to see that they
moved their respective schools around from one locality to another, so that
all the inhabitants of each and every township should have a fair chance
at the 'cultivation of learning and good manners.' Thus from time to
time, as circumstances required, other laws were passed, whose object was
to extend the work, the beginning of which appeared so insignificant; and
in the process of years, educational matters were reduced to something
bearing a resemblance to system. Schools and schoolmasters became, in
time, a necessity; and when, after the revolution, neighboring states

began to make provision for their permanent establishment and maintenance, a desire was also manifested here to do something in the same
direction. Various projects for creating a fund for the support of schools
were discussed, but nothing could be agreed upon that did not call for an
onerous tax upon the people. In the year 1813 the state came into possession of forty thousand dollars, by the sale of certain bank stock which
it was deemed undesirable for her to hold; and the friends of education,
believing this to be a favorable opportunity, undertook to make this surplus
in the treasury a nucleus for a permanent fund for the support of schools.
Mr. James Parker, of Perth Amboy, still among the honored living, was
unwearied in his efforts to secure the appropriation of this money for purposes of education. He introduced into the legislature a resolution to this
effect; but the session being near its close, the subject was postponed,
and, when brought up again during the following year, was once more put
off in consequence of the demands of war. Faithful, however, to the
cause which he had so nobly espoused, Mr. Parker, on his return to the
assembly of 1816–17, again revived the subject, introducing the following
resolution, which was adopted on the 1st of February, 1817.

" 'Resolved, That a committee be appointed to inquire into the expediency of creating a fund for the support of free schools in this state.'

"Placed, according to parliamentary usage, at the head of this committee, he acted with so much promptness that on the fifth of the same month
a bill was reported, entitled 'An act to create a Fund for the Support of
Free Schools,' which was passed by the assembly on the eleventh, and was
introduced into and passed by the council on the twelfth. Thus the
foundation of the school fund of New Jersey was laid."

From the report for the year 1864, of Mr. C. M. Harrison, the state superintendent of public schools, and the annual message, presented in
January, 1865, by Governor Parker, it appears that the total amount
expended in 1864 for school purposes was $637,079.82: that the number
of school buildings was 1,452, of teachers 2,012, and of scholars 149,672.

*Note 16, page 48.*

The suggestion in the text is derived from Yarranton's *England's Improvements*, who, in referring to the success of the Dutch, mentions as one
of its causes, first that "they have fitted themselves with a public register
of all their lands and houses, whereby it is made ready money at all times,
without the charge of law or the necessity of a lawyer." "Thirdly, By a
Public Bank, the great sinews of trade, the credit thereof making paper
go in trade equal with ready money, yea, better, in many parts of the

world than money." He presents this illustration of the system "Now I am a *Dutchman*, and have One hundred pounds a year in the Province of *West-Friezland* near *Groningen*, and I came to the Bank at *Amsterdam*, and there tender a Particular of my Lands, and how tenanted, being One hundred pounds a year in *West Friezland*, and desire them to lend me Four thousand pounds, and I will Mortgage my Land for it. The Answer will be, I will send by the Post to the Register of Groningen your Particular, and at the return of the Post you shall have your Answer. The Register of *Groningen* sends Answer, It is my Land and tenanted according to the Particular. There is no more words, but to tell out your Monies. Observe all you that read this, and tell your children this strange thing, *That Paper in Holland is equal with moneys in* England, I refuse the Moneys, I tell him I do not want Moneys, I want credit, and having one son at *Venice*, one at *Noremberge*, one at *Hamburgh*, and one at *Dantzick*, where Banks are. I desire four Tickets of Credit, each of them for a Thousand pounds, with Letters of Advice directed to each of my sons, which is immediately done, and I mortgage my Lands at three in the hundred. Reader I pray observe, that every Acre of Land in the *Seven Provinces* trades all the world over, and it is as good as ready money: In England * * * many Gentlemen at this day at five hundred pounds a year in Land, cannot have credit to live at a Twelve penny Ordinary. If this be so, it is very clear and evident, that a man with one hundred pounds a year in *Holland*, so convient as their Titles are, and at the paying but three in the hundred interest for the Moneys lent, may sooner raise three families, than a Gentleman in England can either raise one, or preserve the family in being, for the reasons already given. But were the Free Lands of England under a voluntary Register, all these Miseries would vanish, and the land would come to thirty years Purchase, which I shall show you in its proper place * * * I can both in *England* and *Wales* Register my Wedding, my Burial, and my Christening, and a poor Parish Clerk is intrusted with the Keeping of the Book, and that which is Registered there, is good by our Law: But I cannot Register my Land to be honest to pay every man his own, to prevent those sad things that attend families for want thereof, and to have the great benefit and advantage that would come thereby. A Register will quicken trade, and the Land registered will equal as cash in a mans hands and the credit thereof will go and do in trade what ready moneys now doth. Observe how it advanceth trade in Holland, and of how little Advantage it is to the Trade in England. I having one hundred pounds a year in Holland, meet with a Merchant upon the *Exchange* at *Amsterdam* and agree with him for goods to the value of Four thousand pounds for six months. If he demands security I go to the Bank, and give him security

by a ticket of my Land, and by the credit of that Ticket the Merchant is
immediately in Trade again as high as the commodity, was, he sold. But
if I make a Bargain at London for Four thousand pounds worth of Goods
for six months, the next discourse is, what security? Then the Buyer and
the Seller agree to meet at the Tavern at four of the clock in the Afternoon:
There Buyer produceth his security, many times not approved of; so the
Merchant cannot put off his commodities, nor the chapman have the Goods
he stands in need of. But if the Buyer or any Friend of his that would
credit him, had Land under a Register, then a Ticket upon such Lands
given to the Merchant would be equal to him as Ready Moneys; and I say
better too * * * But you will say, I talk that Gentlemen in *England* cannot
have Moneys for Land; It is not so: And that I say Lawyers know no
Titles, I ought to have my pate crackt; for money is plentiful, and Lawyers are cunning enough to spy out good Titles.

"As to both I would it were true for the sake of the poor Gentlemen
and the Lawyers too. But as to the greatest part of them, that have a
Thousand pounds a year, the world knows they are so far from borrowing
Four thousand pounds, that they cannot borrow Four hundred pounds;
and I dare say some Lords also.

"Nay, to my knowledge three eminent Lawyers have been put to much
charge and trouble in their Estates lately purchased by them in Montgom-
ery, Hereford, and Worcester shires by reason of former incumbrances:
Now if an Eminent Lawyer cannot purchase an Estate without so much
trouble, hazard, and charge, upon a Title settled at least Fifty years ago by
all the Judges of England and in the Exchequer chamber; upon what security can the Banks be understood to lay out their moneys safe? And the
poor countrymen are yet in a worse condition. * * * Of late years
the monied Men in England sent their moneys into Lombard street, and
there received a note from a Goldsmith's Boy which was all they had to
shew for their Moneys. And certainly there was a Reason, wherefore
the great monied men did take such slender security for their Moneys:
The Reason was because the Land security was so uncertain and bad, and
it was so troublesome and chargeable getting their Moneys again when
they had occasion to use it, that fore't them to Lombard street."—*Yarranton*, pp. 7, 10, 17.

The embarrassment resulting from the want of a more abundant medium
of exchange, than that afforded by the coin of other countries, and the
still rarer circulation of the Pine Tree currency of New England, issued
by the mint established in Boston in 1652, was early felt in Pennsylvania
and in New Jersey.

Whether the policy of emitting bills of credit was sound or not the public did not lack an opportunity of coming to a judgment, so far as the subject was presented by the pamphlets published, not in Pennsylvania and New Jersey only, but in other portions of the country. No question has, from the beginning of our history, been more thoroughly examined than that of the currency. And although there doubtless were sound reasons to be presented on both sides, we believe no one will refuse to concede that, so far as concerns Pennsylvania and New Jersey, the weight of the argument was in favor of the friends of paper money. Certain it is, that the prosperity of both provinces began very sensibly to increase from the date of the establishment of a loan office, and the issuing of bills of credit. The measure was forced upon the people.

Paper money was first issued in New Jersey in 1709. As the act, authorizing its issue, is not to be found in any of the numerous editions of the laws of that state, and but one copy of it is positively known to exist, we present it without abridgment, and beg to express our obligations to Mr. Charles E. Green, of Trenton, to whose industrious research we are indebted for the transcript.

At a General Assembly held at Burlington from the 13th day of May to the 30th day of June, 1709, in the 8th year of the reign of Queen Anne, the following law was passed:

Chap. XX. An Act for enforcing the Currency of Bills of Credit for Three Thousand Pounds.

Be it enacted by the Lieut. Governor, Council and General Assembly, and by the authority of the same. That Bills of Credit shall be issued forth to the value of £3000, and no more, pursuant to the value of money specified in an act for the support of her Majesty's Government of New Jersey for one year; which Bills shall be in manner and form following, viz:

(This indented Bill of......... shillings, due from the colony of New Jersey to the possessor thereof, shall be in value equal to money, and shall be accordingly accepted by the Treasurer of this Colony, for the time being, in all public payments, and for any fund at any time in the Treasury. Dated, New Jersey, the 1st of July, 1709. By order of the Lieutenant Governor, Council and General Assembly of the said Colony.)

Which Bills shall be signed by Mr. Thomas Pike, Capt. Thomas Farmer, Mr. John Royce and Capt. Elisha Parker, or any three of them, who are hereby appointed and directed to sign the same, and lodge the same in the Treasurer's hands, to be issued out by the Treasurers, under the hands of the said Capt. Thomas Farmer, Mr. John Royce and Capt.

Elisha Parker, or any two of them, for provisions, and every other thing whatever, necessary for and relating to the expedition against Canada; and further to be issued out by the Treasurers, by warrants under the hand of the Lieutenant Governor, or Commander in Chief for the time being, for such pay as shall be due to such Captains and Lieutenants as go on said expeditions according to an act of General Assembly, entitled, An act for encouragement of Volunteers to join the expedition to Canada; and further to be issued out by the said Treasurer, by warrants under the hands of the Captains aforesaid, for payment of such rewards as are given to volunteers who go on said expedition, according to the afore-recited act of General Assembly.

Which Bills shall be received, taken for the value as aforesaid, and equal to the current coyn passing in this colony for goods bought or sold, in any payment to be made for debts contracted, or that shall be contracted; and the tender of the said Bills for the payment and discharge of any debt, or debts, bargains, sales, bonds, Bills, mortgages and specialties whatsoever, shall be as good and effectual in the law, to all intents, constructions and purposes, as if the current coyn of this Colony had been offered and tendered to any person or persons whatsoever, for the discharge of ye same, or any part thereof.

And Be it further enacted, &c. That the said Bills of credit shall be printed and numbered, expressing in every of them the sum of moneys they shall be current for; and to prevent counterfeiting any of the said bills, they shall be dated and indented on the top thereof, with the arms of the Queen of Great Brittain, stampt or printed on the left side thereof, towards the bottom of every of the said Bills; and the indent shall pair with and suit a counterpart thereof, bound in a book for that purpose, and subscribed by the parties herein appointed to do ye same, to be kept by the Treasurers, of the same tenor and date, and so near in similitude, in all circumstances, as possible may be, to such Bills of credit that are issued and made current in payment, as aforesaid. Two hundred of which said bills shall be for £5 each bill; Two hundred of them for forty shillings each; six hundred of them for twenty shillings each; One thousand of them for two shillings each; and Two thousand of them for five shillings each Bill, amounting to, in all, three thousand pounds.

Provided alway, and this the true intent and meaning of this Act. That the said *Signees* shall not sign a quarter number of the said bills of credit than what shall amount to or pass, or be current for more than three thousand pounds money aforesaid.

And be it further enacted, &c. That for the better currency of the said Bills of credit, the Collectors and Treasurers of this Colony, for the time

being, shall, and are hereby required and directed to take and receive all
and every the said Bills, according to the value therein expresssed, with
the proportional advance of Two and a half per cent, on all and every
the said bills that shall be offered and tendered to'them the said Collectors
and Treasurers, for any money due for the first payment of the said
£3,000 Tax; and Five per cent on all and every the bills that shall be
offered and tendered to the sd. Collectors and Treasurers for money due
for the second and last payment of the sd. three thousand pound Tax.
And on their receipt of each payment of the sd. £3,000 Tax, they shall
appoint the person that signed the sd. bills to meet him or them the
sd. Treasurer or Treasurers, who are hereby required and directed to
meet and joyn with him or them to examine and compare the said bills so
to be canceled, as aforesaid, and keep the same on a file, in order to be
further examined by the Governour Council and General assembly, for
the time being, or such as they shall appoint, when filing and requiring
the same.

And be it further enacted, &c. That the said Commissioners or signees,
shall take an oath before any justice of the Peace of this Province, being
of the Quorum, in the words following:

I, A. B., do on the holy Evangelists, sincerely swear, that I will, to the
best of my knowledge and skill, truly, sincerely and faithfully discharge
the trust reposed in me, relating to and concerning the signing and issuing Bills of Credit, mentioned in, and pursuant to ye true intent and
meaning of An act for the enforcing the currency of Bills of credit for
three thousand pounds.

So help me God.

And be it further enacted, &c. That such person or persons as shall be
convicted of Counterfeiting any of the said bills of credit, shall incur the
pains and penalties of Felony, without the benefit of Clergy, and suffer
accordingly.

And be it further enacted, &c. That the said bills of credit shall be current as aforesaid, between man and man, the Treasurers excepted, only
until the first day of June, which will be in the year of our Lord, 1711,
and shall and may be received by the Treasurers until the first day of
September then next following, and no longer.

And be it further enacted, &c. That the Three Thousand pound Tax passed
this session, shall be paid to the said Treasurers in the said Bills of
credit, and in no other specie whatsoever.

In 1716 another act was passed authorizing the creation of about 4,000
pounds proclamation money. In 1723 40,000 pounds were issued, of
which 4,000 were principally applied to the redemption of the old bills.

The remainder it was directed, should be lent on the mortgage of real estate and the deposit of plate. The bills were made on legal tender under heavy penalties for a refusal to take them, and to the period of the revolution about six hundred thousand pounds had been issued.— *Hist. of the early settlement of Cumberland Co., N. J.*, ch. 17 and 18; *Bridgeton Chronicle* of April 15 and 22, 1865. By Hon. Judge Elmer, of the Sup. Ct. of N. J.

We are pleased to state that it is Judge Elmer's purpose to considerably enlarge these interesting sketches and to give them to the public in a more permanent form.

The first act authorizing the creation of bills of credit was passed by Pennsylvania in 1722, and was drawn with great care. The wisdom of its provisions, and the pains taken to guard against fraud placed the scheme upon a firm basis, and secured a confidence in the safety of the issue which for years was unimpaired.

Massachusetts preceded Pennsylvania and New Jersey in the adoption of the new system (*An Historical Account of Massachusetts Currency.* By Joseph B. Felt, Boston, 1839) having in 1690 authorized the creation of paper money.—The necessity of the case suggested the only expedient to avert an inconvenience, and the experiment would doubtless have been originated on this side of the Atlantic, even had examples upon the other not already existed. The Pennsylvania act was entitled "An act for emitting and making current Fifteen Thousand Pounds in Bills of Credit," and the preamble sets forth these reasons : "Forasmuch as through the Extreme scarcity of money the trade of the Province is greatly lessened and the payment of the Public Debts of this Government rendered exceeding difficult and likely so to continue unless some medium in commerce be lawfully made current instead of money, be it," &c. The act is based upon 6th Anne for ascertaining the rates of foreign coin in the loan office, and declared to be intended for the "benefit of the Poor industrious sort of people of the Province at an easy rate of interest to relieve them from the present difficulty they labor under." The security required was of the best description. The trustees were authorized to accept the pledge of plate, and mortgages upon lands, houses, or ground rents free of incumbrance, the estate to be in fee, and in the case of lands or ground rents, to be in value double that of the amount mortgaged, but in the case of houses treble, and the guards against attempts at fraud were judicious.

Eleven thousand pounds were to be issued at five per cent. of which one-eighth of the principal was to be paid annually and no applicant was authorized to receive more than one hundred pounds. The bills were made a legal tender and the refusal to accept them in discharge of debts, &c., worked a forfeiture of the debt, and persons offering land or chattels cheaper for bills than for silver subjected the offender to a penalty. As necessity required, fresh loans were from time to time created, and the province continued to prosper under them. Such was the result of the system in Pennsylvania, so admirably planned and executed that Governor Pownall in his work on the administration of the colonies bestows high praise on the paper system of Pennsylvania.—"I will venture to say," he declares, "that there never was a wiser or a better measure, never one calculated to serve the interests of an increasing country, that there never was a measure more steadily pursued or more faithfully executed for forty years together than the Loan office of Pennsylvania founded and administered by the assembly of that province"—*Younge on Paper Money*, p. 8.

The emission of Pennsylvania paper money was never excessive. In 1759 it reached 185,000, the largest amount in circulation at any one time. The contests which were of so frequent occurrence between the governor and the assemblies, and with the mother country, and the absence of a union of the colonies, rendered the system of bills of credit very unstable. Had it been possible to have devised a permanent and uniform medium of circulation the general progress of the country would have been much in advance of the condition in which it was found at the period of the revolution.

The finances were thrown into confusion by that event, and the expenditures which it involved. An attempt to avoid the misfortunes of the past, and initiate a currency of more general credit and circulation resulted, under the recommendation of Robert Morris, in the incorporation by congress, on the 31st of [December, 1781, of [the Bank of North America, at Philadelphia, which on the 1st April, 1782, also received a charter from Pennsylvania. Such, however, was the effect of the spirit of political faction, that the incorporation by the state was repealed, and pamphlets were written to show that congress, under the confederation, had no power to charter such an institution.

The credit which the loan office had established for itself, induced some to prefer that system to the operation of a bank. The latter, notwithstanding, from year to year gained strength, and the benefit derived was so considerable, that the charter which had been repealed by the Legislature was again conferred, and the Bank of North America. under its perpetual incorporation. derived from the congress of the confederation, exists to this day in undiminished vigor and usefulness, the parent institution of the country.

### Note 17. Page 63.

The reader is referred to a valuable note on the subject of wampum by Mr. Gabriel Furman, at p. 42 of Denton's *Description of New York*. Vol. I of Gowans's *Bibliotheca Americana*.

*Note* 18, *Page* 64.

John Cripps was a person of prominence in the early history of West Jersey. In 1682 he was a justice of peace for the jurisdiction of Burlington and also a member of the assembly. Cripps arrived in 1677 in the ship Kent.

*Note* 19, *Page* 72.

We have never met with a copy of this paper.

**THE END.**

# GOWANS'
# BIBLIOTHECA AMERICANA.

Consisting of a series of reprints of rare old books and pamphlets, relating to the early settlement of North America; namely, History, Biography, Topography, Narrative and Poetry. Each book or pamphlet, reprinted accurately and carefully from the original text, with an Historical Introduction and copious Notes, illustrative, biographical, historical, &c., &c.

No. 1. DENTON, DANIEL.— A brief History of New York, formerly New Netherland (1670). A new edition with copious Notes, by the Hon. Gabriel Furman, New York, 1845, fine paper. $2.50.

No. 2. WOOLEY, CHARLES.— A two years' Journal in New York and parts of its Territories in America (1679). A new edition, with copious Historical and Biographical Notes, by E. B. O'Callaghan, M.D. To match Denton's New Netherland. New York, 1860. $2.50.

No. 3. MILLER, JOHN.— A Description of the Province and City of New York, with plans of the City and several Forts as they existed in the year 1695. New edition, with copious Historical and Biographical Notes, by John Gilmary Shea, LL.D. New York, 1862. $2.50.

No. 4. BUDD, THOMAS.— Good Order Established in Pennsylvania and New Jersey, in America, being a true account of the country; with its produce and commodities there made in the year 1685. A new edition with an introduction and copious Historical and Biographical Notes, by Edward Armstrong, Esq. New York, 1865. $2.50.

The above four books, touching the early history of the New-World, now New York, were all produced by residents at the time on the spot, and witnesses to what they relate. In consequence, like all fragments or large treatises, written by eye-witnesses, they possess an interest and authority not connected with the works of copyists or reproducers. These new editions are vastly enhanced in intrinsic value by the Historical and Biographical Notes, added by their respective editors, all well known as being amply capable of doing justice, as commentators on American subjects. Copies of the original editions of these books are worth $100.

The edition of the small paper copies was quite limited, and only fifty copies each of the large paper were produced. These volumes will hereafter possess a value far exceeding the originals, for this two-fold reason: First, there are but few produced, and second, they constitute as it were, landmarks in the early history of the North American Colonies, as well as divers other parts of the new found land of America.

# GOWANS.

## CATALOGUE

OF

# SCARCE AMERICAN BOOKS,

### FOR SALE AT THE AFFIXED PRICES.

## STORE—115 NASSAU STREET, NEW YORK.

*( Between Ann and Beckman Sts.)*

*" In the dim room upon the sofa lull'd —*
*Wild books strew'd round as thick as wild flowers cull'd —*
*How oft has Spencer's vast and varied lay*
*Chang'd Pain's fierce naps to Paladin and Fay! —*
*Or Falstaff's wit — or Milton's solemn strain,*
*Cheer'd this weak frame and flagging sense again.*
*O books! — O blessings! — could the yellow ore*
*That countless sparkled in the Lydian's store,*
*Vie with the wealth ye lately flung round me —*
*That even farm(fulness of agony*
*With which, beneath the garden's cooling breeze,*
*(July's hot face still flashing through the trees.)*
*Slow stole the fever of Disease away;*
*While bent o'er Tasso's sun-beam written lay,*
*His own Armida in that Bower of Bliss*
*Shut to my heart a renovating kiss,*
*Till with Rinaldo I rush'd forth afar*
*Where loud on Zion burst the Red Cross War."*
                          Manuscript Poem found in MILTON'S WORKS.

*" Visible and tangible products of the past, again, I reckon up to the extent of three: cities, with their cabinets and arsenals; then tilled fields, to either or to both of which divisions roads with their hedges may belong; and thirdly — Books. In which third truly, the last-invented, lies a worth far surpassing that of the two others. Wondrous indeed the virtue of a true book. Not like a dead city of stones, yearly crumbling, yearly needing repair; more like a tilled field, but then a spiritual field; like a spiritual tree, let me rather say, it stands from year to year, and from age to age (we have books that date very number some hundred and fifty human ages); and yearly comes its new produce of leaves (commentaries, deductions, philosophical, political systems; or were it only sermons, pamphlets, journalistic essays), every one of which is talismanick and thaumaturgick, for it can permeate men. O thou who art able to write a book, which once in the two centuries or oftener there is a man gifted to do, envy not him whom they name city-builder, and inexpressibly pity him whom they name conqueror or city burner! Thou too art conqueror and victor; but of the true sort, namely, over the devil: thou too hast built what will outlast all marble and metal, and be a wonder-bringing city of the mind, a temple, and seminary, and prophetic mount, whereto all kindreds of the earth will pilgrim. Fool! why journeyest thou wear sandy, in thy art quarry fiercest, to gaze the stone pyramids of Geeza, or the clay ones of Sacchara? Thou stand there, as I can tell thee, idle and inert, looking over the desert, foolishly enough, for the last three thousand years: but canst thou not even thy Hebrew Bible, or even Luther's version thereof ?"............................................................."THOMAS CARLYLE."*

# CATALOGUE.

ACTS OF CONGRESS. From the First Session 1789 to the 30th Congress 1848–9 both inclusive, wanting 13th Session 1813–14 and the 15th Session 1817–18. 28 vols., 8vo. ½ sheep.
Phila., 1793, and Washington, 1849

A COLLECTION of Sundry Publications, and other Documents in relation to the attack made during the late war, upon the private Armed Brig General Armstrong of New York, commanded by S. C. Reed, on the night of the 26th of September, 1814, at the *Island of Fayal*. By his Britannic Majesty's Ships Plantagenet Seventy-four, Bota Frigate, and Carnation Sloop of War. 12mo, pp. 46. *Privately printed. Presentation copy to Bishop Onderdonk.* $5.
New York, 1833.

ADAMS. F. C. Manuel Pereira; or the Sovereign Rule of South Carolina, with Views of Southern Laws, Life and Hospitality. 12mo, pp. 400, $1.
London, 1852.

ADAMS, HANNAH. A summary history of New England, from the first settlement at Plymouth, to the acceptance of the Federal Constitution, comprehending a general sketch of the American War. 8vo, pp. 516, $4.
Dedham, 1799

ADAMS. JOHN QUINCY. The Jubilee of the Constitution. A discourse delivered at the Request of the New York Historical Society, in the City of New York, on Tuesday, the 30th of April, 1839; being the Fiftieth Anniversary of the Inauguration of George Washington as President of the United States, on Thursday, the 30th of April, 1789. 75 cts.
New York, 1837

"This pamphlet should be read by all parties, and then carefully laid aside, as a work abounding in valuable minute points of historical information, many of which are not to be met with elsewhere. We have here a vigorous sketch of the difficulties which preceded, and of the inefficiency which embarrassed the confederation originally adopted by the states, and a faithful detail of the causes arising from the imperfection of the first league which led to the adoption of our present constitution. What Mr. Adams has thus done could not be so well done, perhaps, by any man living. The circumstances by which he has been surrounded from his boyhood — his intimate connection, private and public, with the leading men of the Revolution — his long continued political career — his industrious habits of observation — his personal identification for nearly half a century with the interests of his subject — all had conspired to assure us that this subject would be skillfully handled, and the discourse itself assures us that, essentially, it is."

ADAMS, JOHN. A Defence of the Constitutions of Government of the United States of America. 3 vols., 8vo, calf, $6.
London, 1787

ADAMS, JOHN (*Second President of the United States*). The works of, with a life of the author. Notes and Illustrations by his Grandson, Charles Francis Adams. Portraits, 10 vols., 8vo, cloth, $20.
Boston, 1850

ALLAN, JOHN. A Catalogue of the Books, Autographs, Engravings, and
Miscellaneous articles, belonging to, prepared by Joseph Sabin,
*Manuscripted, Priced and Named.* 8vo, scarce, $5.
New York, 1864

ALLAN COLLECTION. A Catalogue of, with the Prices that each article
sold for, and buyers' names printed. 2 vols., paper covers, 8vo, $8.
New York, 1864-5

ALTOWAN; or Incidents of Life and Adventure in the Rocky Mountains,
by an Amateur Traveler. Edited by J. Watson Webb. 2 vols., 12mo,
full morocco, gilt, very neat, pp. 255-240, $6. New York, 1846

AMERICAN ALMANAC and Repository of Useful Knowledge, from
1830 to 1860. Paper covers, both inclusive, forming a complete
set. $31. Boston, 1830-60
The above named series of volumes forms the only consecutive annals of the
United States for the last thirty-one years. They possess intrinsic value to all
who would desire accurate information concerning the country during that
period.

AMERICAN INSTITUTE. The Lectures delivered before the Am. Institute of Instruction, including the Journal of Proceedings and a list
of the officers for the years 1840, 42, 44, 45, 46, 47, 48, 49, 50, 51, 52,
54, 55, 56, 57, 58 and 1862. 17 vols., 12mo, $8.50.
Boston, 1841-63

DITTO for the years 1842, 45, 50, 52, 54, 55, 56, and 58. 8 vols., 12mo,
$4.00. Boston, 1843-59

AMERICAN HISTORICAL and Literary Curiosities, consisting of fac-similes
of original documents relating to the Revolution, relics of antiquities and modern autographs. Fol., $7.00. Phil., 1861

AMERICAN LITERARY GAZETTE and Publishers' circular. 4 vols., 8vo,
$8.00. Phila., 1863-65

AMERICAN NEPOS (The). A collection of the Lives of the most remarkable and the most eminent men, who have contributed to the discovery, settlement, and the independence of America. 12mo, pp.
395. $2. Baltimore, 1806

ANNALS OF CONGRESS. The Debates and Proceedings in the Congress
of the United States, with an appendix, containing important state
papers and public documents, and all the laws of a public nature,
with a copious index, compiled by Joseph Gales from 1st congress,
1789-91 to 18th congress 1842. 41 vols., royal 8vo, law sheep, $61.50.
Washington, 1834

DEBATES IN CONGRESS. Register of, comprising the leading debates
and incidents of the 2d session of the 18th congress, together with
an Appendix, containing the most important state papers and public
documents, &c. &c., with a copious Index to the whole, from vol. 1,
1824-5 to 1837, wanting part 1 of vol. 9. 28 vols., royal 8vo, law
sheep, $42. Washington, 1825-38
The above series of volumes with the *Congressional Globe* embraces all the
reported debates which took place in both houses of Congress from the forma-
tion of the government of the U. S. to the present time, as well as important
state papers, public documents and fragmentary pieces. To an aspirant after
political distinction they are indispensable to possess and to study. Thomas
H. Benton in a great measure gathered his wide spread and well merited
distinction as a statesman from having become intimate with their contents.

ANNALS OF SAN FRANCISCO, containing a Summary of the History of the
First Discovery, Settlement, Progress and Present Condition of

California, and a complete History of all the Important Events connected with its Great City, to which are added Biographical Memoirs of some Prominent Citizens, by Frank Soule, John H. Gibson,
M.D. and James Nisbet. Illustrated with 150 fine engravings, royal
8vo, cloth, pp. 824, $2.25.                              New York, 1855

APOLLO ASSOCIATION. Transactions of, for 1839–40 and 41. By-laws
of the Association. Sixth Exhibition Catalogue of 1840. Transactions of the American Art Union, formerly called the Apollo Association, 1847. Catalogue of Paintings and Sculpture at the Apollo
Gallery 410 Broadway, 1839. In all Seven pamphlets. $2.

AUDUBON, JOHN JAMES. Ornithological Biography, or an account of the
habits of the Birds of the United States of America; accompanied
by descriptions of the objects represented in the work entitled
The Birds of America, and interspersed with delineations of American Scenery and Manners. Vols., 2, 3, 4 and 5, royal 8vo, $10.
                                                       Edinburgh, 1834

AUDUBON, JOHN J. A synopsis of the Birds of North America. 8vo,
cloth, pp. 370, $2.00.                                 Edinburgh, 1839

AUDUBON, J. J. The Naturalist of the New World, his adventures and
discoveries, by Mrs. Horace St. John. 12mo, pp. 337, plates. $1.50.
                                                        New York, 1856

AUDUBON, J. J. The Birds of America, from drawings made in the United States and their territories. Vol. 1. royal 8vo, 32 col'd plates,
unbound.                                                New York, 1840

JOHN JAMES AUDUBON, the celebrated American ornithologist, was a French-
man in every sense of the word, with the exception of the place of his birth;
lively, enthusiastic and courteous in the extreme. His enthusiasm, more especially in anything he had placed his mind, was so ardent as to affect his
accuracy, inasmuch as his imagination was much stronger than his judgment,
and such will be the case with all so mentally constituted (enthusiasm and
judgment are like oil and water, incompatible with each other). He was a
native of the United States and the state of Louisiana, which has a climate
so genial throughout the whole year that the indigenous feathered tribes swarm
in incredible numbers, both aquatic and land, with plumage remarkable for
variety and dazzling richness of color, to such a degree that it amounts to the
grandeur of gorgeousness. The youthful and poetical mind of the afterwards
eminent naturalist must have been fired with a love for the study of these
beautiful objects forming this branch of natural history. When I was a dweller
in that part of the south I still remember how the sight of these gaudy winged
creatures affected me, even to enthusiasm; how then must they have affected
one so susceptible to such impressions! No wonder he became the historian of the birds of the new world! It may be said of Audubon, as Horace
has predicted of himself and his writings, namely: "That he has erected to
himself a monument more lasting than brass or marble, which the blasting
north wind cannot destroy, nor even time itself." His great work, the Orni-
thology of North America, is now a book unprocurable, except when a copy may
be found in a private library when disposed of by private or public sale. I
remember selling a copy for $350. I understand that a copy at this time is worth
$1,000, or even $1,200, and as time rolls on the price will advance beyond these
figures. An edition in reduced form has been published by one of his sons,
seven volumes, royal 8vo, which can be purchased for $150. The plates of the
first edition are from copper, while those of the second are lithographed.
There is no comparison between the editions. Besides his great ornithological
work and the reduced editions, he has published an ornithological biography in
five volumes, royal 8vo, and a magnificent work on the quadrupeds of North
America. For a full list of his works see my American Biographical Bibliogra-
phy. In collecting material for his work he traversed as far south as Yucatan
in Mexico, west to the Rocky mountains, north as far as the bleak shores of
Labrador, and east along the coast of North America from the gulf of St.
Lawrence to the Rio Grande, as well as the interior surroundings of these coast

regions. Respecting the sale of this great book, he related the following very interesting narrative which ought never to be lost sight of; it redounds to the everlasting dishonor of certain parties, while it does great credit to that very much abused man, Louis Philippe, king of the French. "I did not sell," said he, "more than forty copies of my work in England, Ireland, Scotland and France, of which Louis Philippe took ten." The following subscribers received their copies but never paid for them. George IV, Dutches of Clarence, Marquis of Londonderry, Princess of Hesse Homburg. An Irish Lord whose name he could not give, took two an I paid for neither. Rothschild paid for his copy, but with great reluctance. The same could be said of a wealthy citizen of the United States. He further said he sold seventy-five copies in America, twenty-six in New York, twenty-four in Bo-ton, that the work altogether cost him £27,000, and that he lost $25,000 by it. He said that Louis Philippe offered to subscribe for one hundred copies if he would publish the work in Paris. This he found could not be done, as it would have required forty years to finish it as things then were in the French capital. His aged and amiable widow still survives (1856). I have learned that she had in her possession a very valuable manuscript, written by those famous travelers, Messrs. Lewis and Clark, who made the first exploring tour from St. Louis to the mouth of the Columbia river. This manuscript is said to be a continuation of the tour already published, and was found in the possession of an Indian or an Indian trader somewhere among the gorges of the Rocky mountains. It no doubt had been stolen from those indefatigable explorers, as it is well known the Indians are great thieves....................................................WESTERN MEMORABILIA.

CLAY, SIDNEY.   Personal Recollections of the American Revolution. A private journal, prepared from authentic domestic records, together with Reminiscences of Washington and Lafayette.   12mo, cloth, $1.50.                                                    New York, 1859

NARD, HENRY.   National Education in Europe; being an account of the organization, administration, &c., of public schools of different grades in the principal states.   Thick 8vo, cloth, $1.50.
                                                                   Hartford, 1854

NARD, HENRY.   The American Journal of Education, edited by. Vols. 3, 4 and 5, containing many fine steel portraits.   3 vols, thick 8vo, $6.75.                                           Hartford. 1858

STOW, GEO.   The History of New Hampshire from its Discovery in 1614 to the Passage of the Toleration Act in 1819.   Second edition, 8vo, cloth, pp. 456, $2.                          Boston and New York, 1853

TLETT, J. R.   Records of the Colony of Rhode Island and Providence Plantations in New England.   5 vols., 8vo, cloth, $10.
                                                                 Providence, 1856

NETT, JAMES GORDON.   Editor of the New York Herald.   Life and Writings of.   8vo, pp. 64 (three caricature portraits).
                                                                   New York. 1844
This pamphlet has been sold at auction as high as six dollars and twenty-five cents.

NETT, JAMES GORDON.   Editor and owner of the New York Herald. Memoirs of his Life and Times, by a Journalist.   12mo, portrait, $1.50.                                               New York, 1855

NETT, JAMES GORDON.   An account of, as well as of his newspaper establishment in the last and expiring volume of the Democratic Review.   $2.                                         New York, 1852

NETT, JAMES GORDON.   Morning Herald, afterwards rebaptized the New York Morning Herald.   Vol. 1st.   From May 6th. 1835, to August 12th, 1835.   In good preservation, very rare, small folio.
                                                                   New York. 1838
The first article in the first number of this publication is a biography of Matthias the prophet, who really was the harbinger of Joe Smith and Mormonism.

[ 6 ]

JAMES GORDON BENNETT. At the birth and during the infant days of the *New York Herald*, nothing could seem more unlikely to survive for any length of time than it did. A sickly child just born, and to all appearances quietly breathing away its existence would appear to be a befitting emblem of its first appearance, and its attempt to walk. The editor and proprietor, without assistance, without means, without friends, a stranger among a strange people, and the paper of very diminutive dimensions, and filled with indifferent matter, with a community not quite ready to be extensive purchasers of a daily morning paper, &c., &c. When all these features are taken into consideration, neither the most sagacious conjecturer nor the keenest eyed seer could have ventured to predict its ultimate success.

I remember to have entered the subterranean office of its editor early in its career, and purchased a single copy of the paper, for which I paid the sum of one cent United States currency. On this occasion the proprietor, editor and vender was seated at his desk busily engaged writing, and appeared to pay little or no attention to me as I entered. On making known my object in coming in, he requested me to put my money down on the counter, and help myself to a paper; all this time he continuing his writing operations. The office was a single oblong underground room; its furniture consisted of a counter, which also served as a desk, constructed from two flour barrels, perhaps empty, standing apart from each other about four feet, with a single plank covering both; a chair, placed in the centre, upon which sat the editor busy at his vocation, with an inkstand by his right hand; on the end nearest the door were placed the papers for sale. This is a faithful sketch as near as I can remember of its editor's humble but interesting apartments. Like all other successful projects, its success may be attributed to a combination of causes, of which I will venture to enumerate the following: First, the editor was born, nurtured, trained and educated in Scotland, an insignificant spot placed upon the hip of the surface of our rolling and shifting globe, in point of size a mere nook, which has produced more men who have distinguished themselves in every department of human exertion than any other subdivision on the face of the earth, ancient Greece alone excepted; a country where the youth is taught to think and act for himself with Spartan firmness, while the steadiest prudence and economy are enforced, not only by precept but by the uniform example of all in authority from the humblest parent upwards. When these qualities are joined with an unyielding perseverance, accompanied with a sound judgment, the result is pretty certain to be a success, no matter what may be the vocation. Many of these characteristics the editor undoubtedly possessed. Second, its cheapness, which threw it within the reach of the humblest citizen. Third, its advertising patronage, which was considerable. Fourth, he early secured the assistance of William H. Attree, a man of uncommon abilities as a reporter, and a concoctor of pithy as well as ludicrous chapters, greatly calculated to captivate the many readers. In fact, this clever and talented assistant in some respects never had his match; he did not, as other reporters do, take down in short hand what the speaker or reader said, but sat and heard the passing discourse like any other casual spectator; when over, he would go home and retire to his room, write out in full all that had been said on the occasion, and that entirely from memory. On a certain occasion I hinted to him my incredulity about his ability to report as he had frequently informed me. To put this matter beyond doubt, he requested me to accompany him to Clinton Hall, to hear some literary magnate let off his intellectual steam. I accordingly accompanied him as per arrangement. We were seated together in the same pew. He placed his hands in his pockets, and continued in that position during the delivery of the discourse; and when finished, he remarked to me that I would not only find the substance of this harangue in the *Herald* to-morrow, but I would find it word for word. On the following morning I procured the paper and read the report of what I had heard the previous evening, and I must say I was struck with astonishment at its perfect accuracy. I say so unhesitatingly, inasmuch as I feel confident that I have a more than ordinary good memory; more especially in being able to retain what I have heard delivered by a public speaker.* Before Mr. Attree's time, reporting for the press in New York was a mere outline or sketch of what had been said or done; but he infused life and soul into this department of journalism. His reports were full, accurate, graphic; and what is more, he

---

* It may be asked how I knew it to be Mr. Attree's report? Mine answer is this: To one acquainted with his style, there was no mistaking it. It was as easily recognized as the styles of Shakespeare, Junius or Thomas Carlyle. William H. Attree died Nov. 25th, 1849, and lies entombed in Greenwood.

frequently flattered the vanity of the speaker by making a much better speech for him than he possibly could himself, thereby killing two dogs with one stone. He captivated the speaker excessively at reading his own speech, and the community was much better satisfied with Mr. Attree's report than they would have been with the author's too often bald and disjointed remarks. These reports, making their appearance in the *Herald* almost daily, added greatly to its circulation, and, as a consequence, to its popularity. Fifth, the editor had the faculty of stimulating opposition among the craft to an unparalleled degree. These colaborers in the same vineyard, not only in the city but far outside of it, would from time to time with great earnestness attack him with a spiteful violence which often sounded to the reader like frenzied fury, pouring out upon him the most infamous, unmanly and unfounded abuse. The most scurrilous and untruthful of these attacks he would reprint in his own paper, and occasionally collect all the most opprobrious epithets applied to him by these journals and set them forth in a solid column of the *Herald*, while always careful to give his authority. These attacks, and his peculiar method of reply, had the effect to add popularity to his own journal in no small degree. The neutral public is certain to sympathize with one whom they see attempted to be hunted down by those pursuing the same course, and displaying no signs of better breeding nor higher standard of action than their intended victim. In the heat of these controversies he at one time obtained the title of the Ishmaelite of the press. Sixth, Dr. Benjamin Brandreth of well and wide-spread reputation, and who has made more happy and comfortable, for a longer or shorter time, as the case may be, by his prescriptions than any other son of Æsculapius, hailed me one day as I jumped from a rail road car passing up and along the shores of the Hudson river, and immediately commenced the following narrative. He held in his hand a copy of the *New York Herald*. "Do you know," said he, holding up the paper to my face, "that it was by and through your agency that this paper ever became successful?" I replied in the negative. "Then," continued he, "I will unfold the secret to you of how you became instrumental in this matter. Shortly after my arrival in America I began looking about me how I was to dispose of my pills by agents and other means. Among others, I called upon you, then a bookseller in Chatham street. After some conversation on the subject of my errand, a contract was soon entered into between us — you to sell and I to furnish the said pills; but, continued he, these pills will be of no use to me or any one else unless they can be made known to the public, or rather the great herd of the people; and that can only be done by advertising through some paper which goes into the hands of the many. Can you point out to me any such paper, published in the city? After a short pause I in substance said that there had lately started a small penny paper, which had been making a great noise during its existence; and I had reason to believe it had obtained a very considerable circulation among that class of people which he desired to reach by advertising, and so concluded that it would be the best paper in the city for his purpose, provided he could make terms with the owner, who, I had no doubt, would be well disposed, as in all probability he stood in need of patronage of this kind. I immediately," continued he, "adopted your advice, went directly to Mr. Bennett, made terms with him for advertising, and for a long time paid him a very considerable sum weekly for the use of his columns, which tended greatly to add to both his and my own treasury. The editor of the *Herald* afterwards acknowledged to me that but for his advertising patronage he would have been compelled to collapse. Hence," said he, "had I never called on you, in all probability I should not have had my attention turned to the *New York Herald*; and, as a consequence, that sheet would never have had my advertising; and that paper would have been a thing of the past, and perhaps entirely forgotten." Seventh, about the year 1830 in London began being published the *Illustrated Penny Magazine*, which was imported into America in large quantities, and sold extensively in New York and other cities of the United States, thereby creating a taste for cheap literature; and it may be said, that out of this publication sprung up the cheap or penny press in America. The first paper of this kind was commenced in January, 1833, named the *Penny Post*. It had but a short existence, but still it was the first penny paper published in America.* Then followed the *Sun*, whose career commenced about nine months after. This, unlike its predecessor, proved successful, mainly from the advertising patronage it had, and

---

* Those curious in authenticating such matters can be gratified with a sight of the early numbers of the first penny paper printed in America at the New York Historical Society's Library, where copies of each have been deposited.

what is more, it still lives healthy and vigorous. Then was brought into existence the *Transcript*, a remarkably spirited little paper, edited for some time by
Dr. Asa Greene, author of the adventures of Dr. Dodemus Duckworth, the
steam doctor. Like the first named, after a few years' existence it died, making
no sign. In chronological order was born the *Morning Herald*, its primitive
title, afterwards rebaptized the *New York Herald*: and this proved to be a
success indeed. From its own showing, it has an aggregate circulation throughout the year of one hundred and twenty-five thousand copies each day, an
income from the sale of the paper of one million ninety-five thousand dollars
yearly, and employs two hundred and thirty-three hands daily, besides a host
of correspondents scattered all over the world: thus having a greater force and
circulation than the combined daily press of New York, and greater than any
other paper in the world, with the exception of the *London Times*: besides,
its editor and owner has in process of construction a printing house mansion,
located at the corner of Ann street and Broadway, which will surpass anything
of the kind in the world.

Thus it will be perceived that the *Herald* had the road pretty well paved for
its reception; in some respects like the civil engineer, who, away in the western
wilds, laying out his route for a rail road, a turnpike or canal, follows the
track of the buffalo that roams through the dense forests and over the vast sea-
like prairies, tracing out paths the easiest of access with mathematical pre-
cision and unerring aim; so much so, than when these rail road constructors
come along, they follow implicitly the lines traced out by that natural and
instinctive engineer, the buffalo.........................WESTERN MEMORABILIA.

BERRIAN, WILLIAM. An Historical Sketch of Trinity Church. New
York. 8vo, plates, pp. 386. $3. New York. 1847

BESS. * * An Abstract of the Sufferings of the People called Quakers
for the Testimony of a Good Conscience. from the time of their being
first distinguished by that name. 3 vols., 8vo, old calf, good order,
$12. London, 1733

BLAKE, W. J. The History of Putnam County, N. Y., with an enumeration of its Towns. Villages, Rivers, Creeks. Lakes, Ponds, Mountains, Hills, and Geological Features. Local Traditions, and short
Biographical Sketches of early settlers. 12mo, cloth. pp. 368, $2.50.
New York. 1849

BLENNERHASSETT PAPERS. The, embodying the private journal of Har-
man Blennerhassett, and the hitherto unpublished correspondence
of Burr. Alston. Comfort Tyler, Deveraux. Dayton, Adair, Miro,
Emmett. Theodosia Burr Alston, Mrs. Blennerhassett. and others,
their cotemporaries. developing the purpose and aims of those
engaged in the attempted Wilkinson and Burr Revolution, &c., &c.,
by William H. Safford. Thick 8vo, cloth, portraits and plates, $4.
Cincinnati, 1864

BLENNERHASSETT, HERMAN. The Life of. comprising an authentic
narrative of the Burr Expedition, and containing many additional
facts not heretofore published by W. H. Safford. 12mo, cloth, $1.50.
Cincinnati, 1853

BLISS. Jr., LEONARD. The History of Rehoboth. Bristol county, Mass.,
comprising a history of the present towns of Rehoboth, Seekonk
and Pawtucket, from their settlement to the present time, with
sketches of Attleborough, Cumberland, and a part of Swansey and
Barrington. 8vo, cloth, pp. 299, $2. Boston, 1836

BOLTON. ROBT. History of the Protestant Episcopal Church in the county
of Westchester, from its foundation, A.D. 1683 to A.D. 1853. 8vo,
pp. 775. 2 portraits and a number of wood cuts, $2. New York, 1855

BOLTON, JR., ROBERT. A History of the County of Westchester. from
its first settlement to the present time. 2 vols., 8vo, cloth. maps, &c.
New York, 1848

:ANT, JOSEPH (Thayendanegea). Life of, including the border wars of the American Revolution, also sketches of the Indian Campaigns of Generals Harmar, St. Clair and Wayne, &c., from the peace of 1783 to the Indian peace of 1795, by William L. Stone. 2 vols., 8vo, cloth, portraits and maps, pp. 531-630, $4.50. Albany, 1864

EWSTER. WILLIAM. Chief of the Pilgrims, or The Life and Times of William Brewster, ruling elder of the Pilgrim company that founded New Plymouth, the Parent Colony of New England, in 1620. By the Rev. Ashbel Steele, A.M. Illustrated with five steel, and four other engravings. $2.50. Phila., 1857

IICK CHURCH MEMORIAL, containing the Discourses delivered by Dr. Spring on the closing of the Old Church in Beekman street, and the opening of the New Church on Murray Hill, the Discourse delivered on the 50th Anniversary, &c., &c. 8vo, plates, cloth, $2.
New York, 1861

ITISH SPY. The Letters of the. Ninth ed., with the last corrections of the author. 18mo, $1. Baltimore, 1831

OWN, HENRY. The History of Illinois, from its first discovery and settlement to the present time, map, 8vo, cloth, pp. 502, $2.25.
New York, 1844

OWN, J. The History and Present Condition of St. Domingo, 2 vols., 18mo, muslin, pp. 307 and 289, $3. Philadelphia, 1837

UE LAWS of New Haven Colony, usually called Blue Laws of Connecticut, Quaker Laws of Plymouth and Massachusetts. Blue Laws of New York, Maryland, Virginia, and South Carolina, &c., &c., compiled by an Antiquarian. 12mo, cloth, $1.25. Hartford, 1838

UDINOT, ELIAS. A Star in the West; or a humble attempt to discover the long lost Ten Tribes of Israel. 8vo, pp. 312, $2. Trenton, 1816

OWN, CHARLES B. (The greatest Am. Novelist), his Novels. 6 vols., 12mo, cloth, $7.50. Phila., 1857

RGH, JAMES. Political Disquisitions; or an Inquiry into Public Errors, Defects, Abuses, illustrated and established upon Facts and Remarks extracted from a variety of Authors, Ancient and Modern. Calculated to draw the timely attention of Government and People to a due Consideration of the necessity, and the means of Reforming the Errors, Defects and Abuses; of Restoring the Constitution and Saving the State. 3 vols., 8vo, $5. London, 1774
Burgh's Political Disquisitions are said to have produced a great effect upon the mind of the American colonists during the revolution. It was published in Philadelphia during the struggle, and extensively circulated throughout the country. Copies of this rare American edition may occasionally be found in the libraries of old American families. On a certain occasion, in my summer wanderings through the lower parts of New Jersey, I fell in with a copy of the American edition; it appeared to be printed on dark brown paper, bound in a very coarse, uncouth style, and altogether had a very primitive appearance. It is recommended by all the leading men of the revolution.—WESTERN MEMORABILIA.

RGESS, HON. TRISTRAM. Battle of Lake Erie, with notices of Com. Elliot's conduct in that engagement. 12mo, cloth, pp. 132, $1.

RGOYNE'S LAMENTATION, a Poem written during the Revolution. 18mo, $1.00. N. D.

RK, JOHN. The History of Virginia from its first settlement to the commencement of the Revolution. 3 vols., 8vo, ½ calf, title to vol. 1 lost, $45. Petersburgh, Va., 1822

2

BURNEY, JAMES. A Chronological History of the Discoveries in the South Sea or Pacific Ocean. 4 vols., 4to, bds., uncut (wants vol. 3), 8G. London, 1803

BURR, AARON. An Examination of the various charges exhibited against Aaron Burr, Esq. By Aristides. 8vo, pp. 59. Virginia, 1804

BURR, AARON. Reports of the Trials of, for Treason, and for a Misdemeanor, in preparing the means of a Military Expedition against Mexico, a territory of the King of Spain, with whom the U. S. were at peace, in the Circuit Court of the U. S. in the city of Richmond, Va., 1807, with an appendix to commit A. Burr, H. Blennerhassett and I. Smith, to be sent for trial to the state of Kentucky, for Treason or Misdemeanor, alleged to be committed there. Taken in short hand by David Robertson. 2 vols., 8vo. Phila., 1808

BURR, AARON. The Private Journal of, during his Residence of Four years in Europe, with Selections from his Correspondence. Edited by Mathew L. Davis. 2 vols., 8vo, pp. 451–453, $4.50. New York, 1836

BURR, AARON. Memoirs of, with Miscellaneous Selections from his Correspondence. By Mathew L. Davis. Portrait and Fac-simile. 2 vols., 8vo, cloth, $4. New York, 1837

BURR, AARON. The Life and Times of. By J. Parton. 12mo, pp. 696, portrait, $2.50. New York, 1858

BURR, AARON. Margret Moncroff, or the First Love of Aaron Burr. A Romance of the Revolution: with an Appendix containing the Letters of Col. Burr to "Kate," "Eliza," and from "Eliza," "Leonora," &c., &c. By Charles Burdett. Fac-simile of one of Burr's Letters. 12mo, pp. 437, $2. New York, 1860

AARON BURR. When a youth navigating the wild Ohio and wilder Mississippi rivers,* I heard of the fame of Aaron Burr and his associates: on these waters were the scenes of some of their exploits. An island in one of these rivers still bears the name of Blennerhasset Island. Shortly after I came to the city of New York Aaron Burr was pointed out to me as he was slowly winding his way up Broadway between Chamber street and the old theatre on the City Hall side. I frequently afterwards met him in this and other streets. He was always an object of interest, inasmuch as he had become a historical character, somewhat notoriously so. I will attempt to describe his appearance, or rather how he appeared to me. He was small, thin, and attenuated in form, perhaps a little over five feet in hight, weight not much over one hundred pounds. He walked with a slow, measured and feeble step, stooping considerably, occasionally with both hands behind his back, small, wrinkled, face, keen, deep set, dark eye, his hat sat deep on his head, the back part sunk down to the collar of the coat and the back brim somewhat turned upwards, dressed in threadbare black cloth, having the appearance of what is known as shabby genteel. His countenance wore a melancholy aspect as well as his whole appearance betokened one dejected, forsaken, forgotten or cast aside and conscious of his position. He was invariably alone when I saw him, except on a single occasion, that was on the side walk in Broadway fronting what is now the Astor House, standing talking very familiarly with a young woman whom he held by one hand. His countenance on that occasion was cheerful, lighted up and bland, altogether different from what it appeared to me when I saw him alone and in conversation with himself. In looking at this fragment of humanity it appeared mysterious to me how he could have become famous in history, social as well as political, or become noted for either good or bad actions of any sort, but again when it is taken into consideration that it is not matter but mind that gives the stamp and produces the wonderful results. HOMER says of one of his heroes that his little body lodged a mighty mind. If we can believe in the Gentoo doctrine of Metempsychosis, it may be that the animating principle which nerved the little Greek hero may have played the same part to the attenuated body of Aaron Burr, when it is taken into consideration that Æsop in body was little more than a head placed upon a lump of shapeless matter, and that Vauban, the renowned French military engineer, appeared on horseback little more than a human head. I remember seeing and hearing in the British house of Commons a certain lord whose appearance might have been taken for Thersites INCARNATE, who was a most graceful and commanding speaker as well as a ready debater. Gen. Hamilton, the greatest mind in the American Revolution, was a small man, and had he lived to the age of his antagonist, would, in all probability, have presented no better appearance. If we may believe Shakespeare up to his time, Richard III was the only real warrior king England ever had. He was sent into the world half made up, and so deformed that the dogs barked at him as he passed them. Pope, the most natural and sweetest of all the English poets, was of diminutive stature as well as very much deformed in figure, (see his full length portrait,) while on the other hand, Alcibiades, Plato, Cicero, Marc Anthony, Brutus, Charlemagne, Peter the Great, Edmund Burke, Robert Burns, Byron, Sir Robert Peel, Professor Wilson (Christopher North), and last, although not least, Daniel Webster, were all remarkably well developed, and presented models of the physical man. In contrasting these opposite classes, it would appear that mind is indifferent as to what kind of lodgings is selected for its habitation, and its operations while connected with the body that perisheth. Burr must have been a very exact man in business transactions. His receipt book came into my possession. I found there, receipts for a load of wood, a carpenter's work for one day, for a pair of boots, milk for a certain number of weeks, suit of clothes, besides numerous other small transactions that but few would think of taking a receipt for. The book was but a sorry cheap affair, and could not have cost, when new, more than fifty cents............WESTERN MEMORABILIA.

*Then there was no by-way for boats to escape the rugged falls of the Ohio as there now is; all had to pass through the yawning straits of Scylla and Charybdis. We had therefore to plunge over unhesitatingly, swifter than an arrow from an Indian's bow, or thought, or lightning, or the soul's departure from the body, the passing over the rapids seems so sudden. These similitudes are not exaggerations but naked truth. Homer has accurately described these falls at low water without having seen them.

"Here Scylla bellows from her dire abodes,
Tremendous pest! abhorr'd by men and gods!
Hideous her voice, and with less terrour roar
The whelps of lions in the midnight hour,
Twelve feet deform'd and foul the fiend dispreads;
Six horrid necks she rears, and six terrific heads;
Her jaws grin dreadful with three rows of teeth;
Jaggy they stand, the gaping den of death;
Beneath, Charybdis holds her boist'rous reign
'Midst roaring whirlpools, and absorbs the main;
Thrice in her gulfs the boiling seas subside,
Thrice in dire thunders she refunds the tide."...................HOMER.

Not a house stood upon the point of land formed by the junction of the Ohio and Mississippi rivers, nor was the land even under cultivation but in its primitive wild, dreary solitude. I understand it is now the site of a large, busy city (Cairo). Seventy miles below, on the west bank of the Mississippi, stood the deserted village of New Madrid, consisting of a few log houses apparently empty, and the surrounding forest all dead, caused, as I learned, by an earthquake a few years ago. The land at this place sunk ten feet from the effects of the shock, and no doubt the concussion caused these monarchs of the forest to wither and die. Fifty miles still further down stood the now city of Memphis. The captain of our sluggish moving boat landed at this place. I accompanied him up the bank, the river being low at the time, for the purpose of buying a supply of whisky. The town I remember consisted of scattered log houses inhabited apparently by a very poor class of people. After falling down below this town about fifty miles we met with no settlement till we reached the vicinity of Walnut Hill, now Vicksburgh, the distance being about six hundred miles. The only music in the day time which regaled our senses was the puffing and distressed moaning of the high pressured steamers which occasionally passed up and down the river, as the case might be, and as an afterpiece the wild screaming of the numerous flocks of paroquets which travel along the bank of the river after descending to a certain latitude, and in the night the wolf's wild howl, not on Onolaska's shore, but the banks of the gloomy and solitary Mississippi. The only human beings we fell in with during this descent, which took six weeks, were certain roving half civilized whites who had pitched their tents at certain points for the purpose of cutting and preparing fuel for the steam boats passing up and down, and numbers of the native sons of the forest who could be seen every now and then paddling their light canoes close into the shore if ascending, and on the contrary in the centre of the river if downwards bound. At first these savage faced painted men somewhat alarmed me; but they frequently paid us a visit by coming along side and on board of our lazy craft. After becoming somewhat familiar with these grim, black haired, half naked fellow beings, I began rather to like them, and wished for their frequent return to break up our monotony. They left the impression on me that they were both generous and confiding. A party came on board one day; one of them could speak a little English; he informed us that one of their number was condemned to death for having murdered one of the tribe when intoxicated. We urged him to make his escape as he appeared to be at liberty; we even offered to take him with us in our boat.

but they all declared, as we could understand them, that that would be of no use, for in the event of his non-appearance for execution on the day appointed, his wife or one of his children would have to suffer in his stead. The three great rivers which discharge their heavy contents into the Mississippi, the Arkansas, the Yazoo and the Red rivers, at these points where they lost themselves in the great father of waters, were all solitary, heavy timbered wildernesses; not a human being appeared to have disturbed their native wild grandeur. Now I understand that at each and all of these points are busy towns, and likely to become large cities. At this time, according to his biographers, Abraham Lincoln must have been a fellow boatman with me on these rivers, although I never saw him to my knowledge. I remember seeing the sons of Morris Birkbeck, the famous Illinois farmer, who published two volumes on the United States.

BUTLER, MANN. A History of the Commonwealth of Kentucky. Port., 8vo., $2.  Louisville, Ky., 1834

CALDWELL, CHARLES, Autobiography of, with a Preface. Notes and Appendix, by Harriot W. Warner. Portrait, 8vo, cloth, pp. 454, $1.50.
Philadelphia, 1855

CALIFORNIA. A Series of Charts with Sailing Directions, embracing surveys of the Farallones, entrance to the Bay of San Francisco, San Pablo, Straits of Carquines and Suisun Bay, Confluence and Deltic Branches of the Sacramento and San Joaquin rivers, and the Sacramento river (with the middle fork) to the American river, including the cities of Sacramento and Boston, state of California, by Cadwalader Ringgold, Commander, 4th Ed., with additions. Maps and plates, small folio, cloth, $2.  Washington, 1852

CANADA. Appendix to Report of the commissioner of Crown Lands. Maps of Canada. Containing 8 large folding maps. 4to, $5.
Toronto, 1857

CAREY, M. The Olive Branch; or Faults on Both Sides, federal and democratic, a serious appeal on the necessity of mutual forgiveness and harmony. 7th ed., 8vo, old calf, $5.  Phila., 1815

CARROLL, B. R. Historical Collections of South Carolina; embracing many Rare and Valuable Pamphlets and other Documents, relating to the History of that State, from its first Discovery to its Independence, in the year 1776. Compiled with various notes and an introduction. 2 vols., 8vo, maps, cloth, scarce, $10.  New York, 1826

CARTER, II. N. Letters from Europe, comprising the Journal of a Tour through Ireland, England, Scotland, France, Italy and Switzerland, in the years 1825, '26 and '27. 2 vols., 8vo, calf, pp. 528–578, $4.
New York, 1827

CARVER, I. Travels through the interior parts of North America, in the years 1766, 1767 and 1768. 3d Edition, to which is added some account of the author, and a copious index. 8vo, half calf, neat, pp. 376. Portrait, maps and plates, $3.  New York, 1838

CASS, GENERAL LEWIS. Sketch of the Life and Public Services of, with the Pamphlet on the Right of Search, and some of his Speeches on the great Political Questions of the Day, by William T. Young. 8vo, cloth, pp. 420, $1.  Detroit, 1852

CATLIN, GEO. Adventures of the Ojibbeway and Ioway Indians in England, France and Belgium; being Notes of Eight Years' Travels and Residence in Europe with his North American Indian collection, with numerous engravings, third edition. 2 vols. in 1, 8vo, cloth, pp. 660, $3.50.  London, 1852

CASTILLO, CAPT. BERNAL DIAZ DEL. The True History of the conquest of Mexico, written in the year 1568. Translated from the original Spanish, by Maurice Keatinge, Esq. 4to, calf, map, $4.00.
London. 1800

CAULKINS, MISS F. M. History of Norwich, Connecticut, from its settlement in 1660, to Jany., 1845. 12mo, pp. 359, plates, $2.
Norwich. 1845

CENSUS. Aggregate amount of each description of Persons in the United States and their territories, according to the Census of 1820. 8vo. pp. 49, $1.
1820

CHAMPLAIN VALLEY. Pioneer History of the, being an account of the settlement of the town of Willsborough by William Gilliland, together with his journal and other papers, and a memoir, and historical and illustrative notes, by William C. Watson. 8vo, paper, $2.50.
Munsell, Albany, 1863

CHARLESTON. Ordinances of the City Council of, in the State of South Carolina, passed since the incorporation of the City, by Alex. Edwards, &c. 4to (no cover), pp. 524, $10.
Charleston, 1802

CHART of the Diocese of New York, from 1830 to 1850, by the Rev. John Frederick Schroeder, D.D., exhibiting in a Map of the thirty-one Counties in the Diocese, all the places where are situated its Churches and Missionary Stations, &c., &c., &c. 4to, colored, 75 cts.

CHEEVER, GEO. B. Punishment by Death, its Authority and Expediency. 12mo, cloth, pp. 110, $1.
New York. 1855

CHEEVER, GEORGE B. The Journal of the Pilgrims at Plymouth, in New England, in 1620. Reprinted from the original volume, with Historical and Local Illustrations of Providences, Principles, and Persons. 12mo, pp. 369, $1.25.
New York, 1848

CHILDS, MRS. L. M. Letters from New York. Amongst much other curious matter about New York will be found an interesting account of McDonald Clark, the poet. 2 vols., 12mo, $2.
N. Y., 1845

CHRISTIAN SPECTATOR. The, conducted by an association of Gentlemen, from vol. 1, 1819, to vol 15, 1833. 15 vols., 8vo, ½ bound. $10.
New Haven. 1819–33

CINCINNATI LITERARY GAZETTE (The). Vols. 1 and 2. Jany. to Dec. 25, 1824. Among the contributors are Dr. Caldwell, C. S. Rafinesque, J. G. Percival, Rembrandt Peale, and an Ancient History of Ohio. This is without doubt the first literary paper published west of the Alleghany Mountains. 4to. pp. 416, $5.
Cincinnati, 1824

CLAPP, JR., WM. W. A Record of the Boston Stage. 12mo, cloth, $1.25.
Boston, 1853

CLARKE, JOSHUA V. B. Onondaga; or Reminiscences of Earlier and Later Times; being a Series of Historical Sketches relative to Onondaga. With notes on the several Towns in the County and Oswego. Map and nine portraits. 2 vols., 8vo, pp. 402 and 393, $6.
Syracuse. N. Y., 1849

CLARK, SAMUEL A. The Episcopal Church in the American Colonies. The History of St. John's Church, Elizabeth Town, New Jersey, from the year 1703 to the present time. 12mo, cloth. pp. 203, wood cuts, $1.
Phila., 1857

CLARK, THOMAS. Naval History of the United States, from the commencement of the Revolutionary war to the present time. 2d ed., very scarce. 2 vols., 12mo, 86. Phila., 1814

CLAY, HENRY. The Life, Correspondence, and Speeches of, by Calvin Colton, LL.D. 6 vols., 8vo, sheep, $15. New York, 1857

CLAY. HENRY. The Last Seven Years of the Life of, by Calvin Colton, LL.D. 8vo. cloth, pp. 504, $2. New York, 1856

CLAY, HENRY. Life and Times of, by Calvin Colton. 2 vols.. 8vo, cloth, port., $3. New York, 1846

CLAY, HENRY. Life and Speeches of, Compiled and Edited by Daniel Mallory, with valuable additions, &c., also various important Letters not heretofore published. 2 vols., thick, 8vo, port., ½ calf, neat, $5. Full cloth, $3. New York, 1857

COAST SURVEY. Report of the Superintendent of the, showing the progress of the Survey during the years 1852–53–54–55–56–57–58–59–60–61 and 1862. Embracing a vast assemblage of reliable local marine maps of creeks, inlets, sandbars, reefs, headlands, river-mouths, harbors, bays and seaports along the Atlantic coast of North America. To an enemy during a war with America these volumes would be worth millions! To America in peace or war they are above all price. 12 vols., 4to, cloth, $24. Washington, 1853–64

COLDEN, CADWALLADER D., Memoir. Prepared at the Request of a Committee of the Common Council of the city of New York, and presented to the Mayor of the city, at the Celebration of the Completion of the New York Canals. 4to, pp. 406, half calf, 5 portraits; 34 plates; 5 maps; 12 fac-simile letters, $10. N. Y., 1825

COLE THOMAS. The Life and Works of, By Lewis L. Noble. Third ed., 12mo, pp. 415, $2.50. New York, 1856

COLE, like Zeuxis, Cellini, and Gainsborough, was a self taught artist. How they, with many others, came by their intuitive excellence in art, the uninitiated public so far have never been sufficiently informed. He was an Englishman by birth and an American by adoption. At an early period of his life, his father immigrated to America, and took up his abode at Steubensville, on the banks of the Ohio, where he must have imbibed a taste for the natural beauties of American scenery and the study of the fine arts, which afterwards proved of vast importance to him in his profession. Before he reached manhood his father with all his family removed to the city of New York, the heart of the United States, where his genius was fostered, and rendered national by a discriminating and generous public. No artist in America won public favor and obtained celebrity so suddenly as he did, but alas, the grim messenger soon nipped the early blossom. He was born in 1801, and died in 1847. I knew the father of Cole intimately at that time. He was a bookseller in the city of New York in a very humble way, where he pursued that business for a number of years. If ever the mantle of Nathanael fell upon any of our race, justly and appropriately I will say, it was upon him. A more primitive, pure and single-hearted man could not well be conceived. "His failings leaned to virtue's side." How delightful would society be if all members of the human family were constituted as he was and acted as he did! The Millenium would be accomplished, Sir Thomas More's Utopia would become a reality, the happy islands in the watery waste easily be reached without any leaving his house and home. I have reason to believe that the artist was fortunately endowed with the like amiable virtues of his venerable father. It was mainly through his instrumentality that I became a bookseller. He let me into all the little knowledge he had of the profession, how he purchased and what profits he made &c, &c. Inasmuch as I had a great hankering after books I devoured up his discourse with a greedy ear, and so adopted the profession...........WESTERN MEMORABILIA.

COLLINS, LEWIS. Historical Sketches of Kentucky ; embracing its History. Antiquities, and Natural Curiosities, Geographical, Statistical, and Geological Descriptions. With Anecdotes of Pioneer Life, and more than *one hundred Biographical Sketches* of distinguished Pioneers, Soldiers, Statesmen, Generals, Lawyers, Divines, &c. Illustrated by forty engravings and a map. 8vo, pp. 560, $6.50.
Cincinnati, 1850

COLUMBUS. Colleccion de los Viages y Descubrimientos, que Hicieron por Mar Los Espanoles desde fines del siglo XV. Con varios documentos inéditos concernientes á la historia de la Marina Castellana y de los estabelecimientos Espanoles en Indias, Coordinada E Illustrada. Por Don Martin Fernandez De Navarrete. 2 vols., fol., large paper, map, uncut, $25.
Madrid, 1825

CONGRESSIONAL GLOBE. From Vol. 8, 26th Congress 1st Session 1839 and 40, to 35th Congress 2d Session 1858-9, including vol. 6 Extra Globe, wanting the following: 1st Session 27th Cong., all of 28th Cong., and 2d Session of 34th Cong. 38 vols., 4to, $50.
Washington, 1839-1859

COOPER, JAMES FENIMORE. Memorial of — with a beautiful portrait of Cooper. 8vo, cloth, pp. 106 $1.50.
New York, 1852

CRAIG, NEVILLE B. The History of Pittsburgh, with a brief notice of its facilities of communication and other advantages for commercial and manufacturing purposes, with two maps. 12mo. cloth, $1.50.
Pittsburgh, Pa., 1851

CRAYON SKETCHES, by an amateur, edited by Theodore S. Fay. 2 vols, 12mo, cloth, $3.
New York, 1833

CROTON AQUEDUCT. KING, CHARLES. A Memoir of the construction, cost, and capacity of the Croton Aqueduct, compiled from official documents, together with an account of the Civic Celebration of the 14th October, 1842, on occasion of the completion of the great work, preceded by a Preliminary Essay on Ancient and Modern Aqueducts. 4to, cloth, plate, pp. 315, $5.
New York, 1843

CROTON AQUEDUCT. TOWER, F. B. Illustrations of the Croton Aqueduct by, of the engineer department. 4to, pp. 152, 22 plates.
New York and London, 1843

CROTON AQUEDUCT. Report of the Commissioners, under an act of the legislature of this state passed Feb. 26th, 1833, relative to supplying the city of New York with pure and wholesome water, Nov., 1833. 8vo, pp. 55, 4 large maps, $3.
New York, 1833

CROTON AQUEDUCT. Report of the Croton Aqueduct Department, made to the common council of the city of New York, for 1850 – 1851 – 1852. 3 vols., 8vo, cloth, $5.
New York, 1851 –'53

CROTON AQUEDUCT. Description of, by John B. Jervis. 8vo, pp. 31, 50 cents.
New York, 1842

CROTON WATER. A volume of Pamphlets and Reports on. Maps and plates, 8vo, $6.
New York, 1833, &c.

CROTON WATER. Spring Water versus Rain Water for supplying the city of New York. Large 8vo, pp. 50, $1.
New York, 1835

CROTON AQUEDUCT. Report of Col. DeWitt Clinton to the Committee on Fire and Water in regard to supplying the city of New York with water. 8vo, pp. 100, $1.50.
New York, 1832

CROTON AQUEDUCT. SCHRAMKE. Description of the New York Croton Aqueduct in English, German and French, with 20 plates. Second edition, 4to, pp. 62, $6. New York and Berlin, 1855

The author was a military engineer in the Prussian service. He obtained a furlough for three years about 1837. During that period, like a prudent man as he was, he made a visit to the United States, and made his headquarters, the city of New York. At that time the Croton Aqueduct was in the process of construction. He made application to the commissioners of that department for employment as an engineer to aid in completing that work, and was accepted. During the time he remained in their employment he filled up his leisure hours in making this book, and on his return to his native country had it published, the text in three languages. Mr. Peter Hastie, the most gifted man connected with the construction of this great national monument, who was well acquainted with this Prussian officer, as well as his ability as an engineer, informed me that Mr. Schramke was an able and faithful assistant, and his book was a scientific performance, and could be relied on by all who desired information of the kind that it treated on.................................. WESTERN MEMORABILIA.

CURWIN. JUDGE. Letters and Journal of Occurrences from 1776 to 1784, with Biographical Notes of Am. Loyalists. 8vo, portrait, $2.
New York, 1842

CYCLOPEDIA of American Literature. By Evert A. Duyckinck and George L. Duyckinck. A review of. 8vo, pp. 32. Privately printed; very scarce. $1 25. N. York, 1856

The author, Dr. R. W. Griswold, on presenting me with a copy of this book said that he considered the Encyclopedia by the brothers Duyckinck a very imperfect performance, while he at the same time admitted the design to be good as well as praiseworthy. He said that he had produced this critique at very considerable expense and research. He professes to have discovered a vast number of errors historical, biographical, and grammatical, besides omissions and commissions and blunders of divers kinds innumerable and unpardonable. But it would be no difficult task to come behind the critic and take up his own text and convict him of the like errors and blunders that he charges upon the authors of the Encyclopedia. I will give a few examples. He states that William Leggett, the American Junius, set up part of the type of his volume of poems entitled the Leisure Hours at Sea. This was a mistake, but he, Leggett, set up the type, printed, and bound a volume of poems which he produced while a resident in the state of Illinois about 1823. This volume was never published, and it is perhaps the rarest of all volumes of American poetry that have ever been printed. The doctor found fault for embracing a number of names as unworthy of being enrolled in the temple of fame. I will name a few of those objected to, namely: McDonald Clarke, the poet; J. D. Hammond, author of the Political History of New York; Robert Coffin, the Boston Bard, and many others of a like standing, and finds fault with their omitting a large list of authors greatly inferior in reputation to those whom he thinks ought to be excluded; but I apprehend that, like Ward's Errata to the Protestant Bible, both were in reality produced for the purpose of bringing the parent publications into contempt. Neither so far as I can learn have succeeded, notwithstanding a certain amount of good may have resulted from both publications."
WESTERN MEMORABILIA.

DARNELL, ELIAS. A Journal containing an accurate and interesting account of the hardships, sufferings, battles, defeat, and captivity of those heroic Kentuckey Volunteers and Regulars, commanded by General Winchester, in the years 1812-13, also two Narratives. 18mo, pp. 99, $1. Phila., 1854

DAVENPORT. IOWA. Past and Present; including the early history, and personal and anecdotal Reminiscences of Davenport, &c., by F. B. Wilkie. Many portraits and plates. 8vo, cloth, $2. Davenport, 1858

DARTMOOR PRISON. The Prisoners' Memoirs, or Dartmoor Prison; containing a complete and impartial history of the entire captivity of the Americans in England, from the commencement of the last war between the United States and Great Britain, until all prisoners were released by the treaty of Ghent. Also, a particular detail of all occurrences relative to the Horird Massacre at Dartmoor on the fatal evening of the 6th of April, 1815. The whole carefully compiled by a Prisoner in England, who was a captive during the whole war. 12mo, pp. 152, $1.50. Printed for the Author. N. Y., 1852

DAVIT, N. S. History of the American Medical Association from its organization up to January, 1855, to which is appended Biographical Notes with nine portraits of the Presidents of the Associations, and of the Author. Edited by S. W. Butler, M.D. 8vo, cloth, pp. 161, $1. Philadelphia, 1855

DEANE, JAMES. Ichnographs from the Sandstone of Connecticut River. 4to, cloth, 46 plates, $5. Boston, 1861

DE FOREST, JOHN W. History of the Connecticut from the Earliest Known Period to 1750, published with the sanction of the Connecticut Historical Society, with a map and illustrations. 12mo, cloth, pp. 53, $2. Hartford, 1853

DEMOCRATIC REVIEW from vol. 1, 1837 and 8, to vol. 30, 1852. Complete, containing over 100 portraits. 30 vols., unbound, or rather in numbers, $100. 1837-52

The *Democratic Review* commenced being published in October, 1837, and ended December, 1852, making in all 174 numbers. About one hundred portraits of men more or less distinguished in the Democratic ranks accompanies the work, with short biographical notices. Complete sets of the Magazine are now unprocurable, except by laborious research in picking up a number or volume from time to time, and these are generally robbed of the plates.

DE ROSS, FRED FITZGERALD. Personal Narrative of Travels in the U. S. and Canada in 1826, illustrated by plates with remarks on the present state of the American Navy. 8vo, bds., plates, $2.50. London, 1827

DE SMET, P. J. (Society of Jesus). Oregon Missions and Travels over the Rocky Mountains in 1845-46. 12mo, plates, pp. 408, $3. New York, 1847

DE WITT, THOMAS (D D.). A Discourse delivered in the North Reformed Dutch Church (collegiate) in the city of New York, on the last Sabbath in August, 1856. 8vo, plates, $2. New York, 1857

DICKINSON, JOHN (Late President of the state of Delaware and of Pennsylvania). The Political Writings of. 2 vols., 8vo, sheep, $10. Wilmington, Da., 1801

Dickinson was one of the most efficient promoters of the American Revolution. His letters signed Fabius were written and published to stimulate the public mind, to acquiesce in and adopt the Federal Constitution. They consequently form an appropriate pendant to the Federalist. In his political opinions he was a consistent advocate of a republican form of government, and in his religious dogmas and practices was a disciple of George Fox and Wm. Penn. He was born in Maryland, December, 1732, and died in Philadelphia, Feb. 15, 1808.

DIPLOMATIC CORRESPONDENCE of the American Revolution, being the letters of Benjamin Franklin, Silas Deane, John Adams, John Jay, Arthur Lee, Wm. Lee and others, together with the letters in reply, &c. Edited by Jared Sparks. 12 vols., 8vo, sheep, $24. Boston, 1829

DISH OF FROGS (The). A Dramatic Sketch, Presented to his Royal Highness, the Prince of Imu. By Monsieur Soupetard. 18mo. pp. 28, 81.
New York, 1839

DIX, JOHN A. Speeches and Occasional Addresses by. 2 vols., 8vo, clo, portrait, 84.50. New York, 1864

DOANE, GEORGE WASHINGTON. The Life and Writings of, for 27 years Bishop of New Jersey, containing his poetical works. sermons, and miscellaneous writings, with a memoir, by his son Wm. C. Doane. 4 vols., 8vo, 88. New York, 1861

DOCUMENTARY HISTORY of the Colony and State of New York. Arranged under the direction of Hon. C. Morgan, by E. B. O'Callaghan, M.D. 4 vols., 8vo, pp. 792–1211–1215–1169. portraits 29, maps 30, plates 32, 86. Albany, 1849–52
The subjects treated of in this truly valuable collection are as follows, namely: Accounts of early settlers; Indian biography, history, difficulties; biographical and genealogical accounts of families; early tours into various parts of the country; statistical accounts; land titles; the Leisler papers; Sir William Johnston's papers; the Rumsey and Fitch Steam boat controversy: churches, wars, disputes, &c., &c., all taken from the manuscript archives of the state. The maps, seals and coins are particularly worthy of attention. These volumes ought to have a place in every public library in the United States.

DOW, LORENZO (the American Diogenes). His whole works, Theological, Historical, Poetical; Travels in England and America, Defence of Camp meetings, &c. 8vo, sheep, 82. Cincinnati, 1854

DRAKE, SAMUEL G. History and Antiquities of Boston, the Capital of Massachusetts, and the Metropolis of New England, from its first settlement in 1630 to 1770. Also an Introductory History of the Discovery and Settlement of New England. Royal 8vo, pp. 800, with numerous plates, fac-similes, pedigrees, &c., half morocco, marbled leaves, 88. Boston, 1856

DUCHE, JACOB (M.A.). Discourses on various Subjects. 3d ed. To which are added 2 Discourses preached at the Chapel of the Asylum, now first published. 2 vols., 8vo. calf. 84. Lond., 1790
"DUCHE, like Galloway, a colaborer in the early career of the Revolution, was supposed to be a firm supporter of the cause, and in consequence was appointed chaplain to the Continental Congress, but subsequently, from fear or some other less laudable reason, and so like many others at that time. put his hand to the plough and looked back, and abandoned the cause."

DUNBAR, E. E. Mexican Papers. The Mexican Question. the Great American Question, with Personal Reminiscences. A Serial issued semi-monthly. 4 Nos., 1 vol., 8vo. cloth. pp. 175. 81.25.
New York, 1860–1

DUNLAP, WILLIAM. History of the New Netherland Province of New York. now State of New York. to the adoption of the Federal Constitution. 2 vols., 8vo, pp. 487 and 528, 86. New York, 1840

DWIGHT, TIMOTHY. Travels in New England and New York. Illustrated with Maps and Plates. 4 thick vols., 8vo, half calf. Nice library set, 86; bds., 85. 1823
A most interesting and valuable work on the Physical Geography, Scenery, Natural History, including Geology, Mineralogy, &c., Vegetation, Government, Notices of Eminent Literary men and others, of the United States.

EATON. GEN. WM. The Life of, several years an officer in the United States army, &c., &c., principally collected from his correspondence and other manuscripts. 8vo, old calf, pp. 448. 82. Brookfield, 1813

EAGER, SAMUEL W. An Outline History of Orange county, with an enumeration of the names of its towns, villages, rivers, creeks, lakes, ponds, &c., and other known localities, biographical sketches of early settlers, etc. 8vo, cloth, $5. Newburgh, 1846

EDINBURGH REVIEW or Critical Journal, from vol. 1 to 48, with an Index. 49 vols., 8vo, ½ bound. 62½ cts. per vol. Edinb., 1804–28

EDWARDS, PRESIDENT. The Works of, with a Memoir of his Life. 10 vols., 8vo, port., $15. New York, 1829

ELLIOTT, CHARLES W. The New England History from the discovery of the continent by the Northmen, A. D. 986, to the period when the colonies declared their Independence, A. D. 1776. 2 vols., 8vo, cloth, 86. New York, 1857

EVANS, OLIVER. The Young Millwright and Miller's Guide, in five parts, embellished with 25 plates. 8vo, pp. 440, 83. Phila., 1795

EXAMINER (The). Containing Political Essays on the most important events of the time, Public Laws and Official Documents. Barent Gardenier, Esq., editor. 5 vols., royal 8vo, $12 50. N. Y., 1814–16

FEDERALIST (The), on the New Constitution, written in 1788, by Mr. Hamilton, Mr. Madison and Mr. Jay. With an Appendix, containing the Letters of Pacificus and Helvidius on the proclamation of neutrality of 1793; also, the original Articles of Confederation, and the Constitution of the United States. New edition. 8vo, sheep, pp. 496, $2.25. Hallowell, 1852

FERRIS's History of the Original Settlements on the Delaware, with History of Wilmington. 8vo, cloth, many fine plates, clean copy, $3. Wilmington, 1846

FILSON, JOHN. The Discovery, Settlement and Present State of Kentucky, and an essay towards the topography and natural history of that important country; to which is added Adventures of Daniel Boon, Minutes of the Piankashaw Council, Account of the Indian Nations, &c., &c., &c. 2 vols., 12mo, map, 85. New York, 1793

FINANCES. Reports of the Secretary of the Treasury of the United States, prepared in obedience to the act of May 10, 1800; to which are prefixed the reports of Alexander Hamilton on Public Credit, A National Bank, Manufactures, and the Establishment of a Mint, from 1790 to 1836. 3 vols., 8vo, law sheep. 89. Washington, 1837

FLANDERS, HENRY. The Lives and Times of the Chief Justices of the Supreme Court of the United States. 8vo, cloth, pp. 645, $2. Philadelphia, 1855

FLORIDA, LA. Del' Inca. Historia del Adelantado Hernando De Soto, Governador, y Capitan General del Reino de la Florida. Y de Otros Heroicos Caballeros, Españoles, E. Indios; escrita por el Inca Garcilasco de la Vega, Cabeca de los Reinos, y Provincias del Peru. Dirigida a la Reina Nuestra Señora. Con Enmendadas en esta impresion, muchas erratas de la Primera. Y añadida Copiosa Tabla de las Cosas Notables. Y el Ensaio Cronologico, que contiene las sucedidas, hasta en el año do. 1722. Vellum, fol., $10. Madrid, 1723

FORD, THOMAS. A History of Illinois, from its commencement as a state in 1818 to 1847, containing a full account of the Black Hawk war, &c., &c. 12mo, pp. 447, 82. Chicago, 1854

**Foote, Wm. Henry.** Sketches of Virginia, Historical and Biographical. 8vo, cloth, pp. 596, $2.50. Phila., 1855

**Force, Peter.** American Archives, consisting of a collection of authentic records, state papers, debates, and letters and other notices of public affairs; the whole forming a Documentary History of the Origin and Progress of the North American Colonies; of the causes and accomplishment of the American Revolution, and of the Constitution of Government for the United States to the final ratification thereof. In 9 vols., large folio, half russia, $50. Washington, 1848

**Forrest, William S.** Historical and Descriptive Sketches of Norfolk and Vicinity, including Portsmouth and the adjacent counties, during a period of two hundred years; also, Sketches of Williamsburgh, Hampton, Suffolk, Smithfield and other places, with descriptions of some of the principal objects of interest in Eastern Virginia. 8vo, pp. 496, $2. Phila., 1853

**Forrest, Edwin.** Report of the Divorce Case of, containing the full and unabridged testimony of all the witnesses, the affidavits and depositions, together with the Consuelo and Forney letters. 8vo, pp. 185, $1. New York, 1852

**Forrest, Edwin.** A Rejoinder to the Replies from England, &c., to certain statements circulated in this country respecting Mr. Macready, together with an Impartial History and Review of the Lamentable Occurrences at the *Astor Place Opera House* May 10th, 1849. By an American Citizen. 8vo, pp. 119, $1.50. New York, 1849

In this pamphlet will be found a review of the difficulties between Macready and Forrest, letters from both parties, history of the riot at the Astor Opera House, coroner's inquest, and other curious historical fragments.

**Forrest, Edwin.** Oration delivered on the Democratic Republican Celebration of the *Sixty-second* Anniversary of the Independence of the United States in the City of New York, July 4, 1838. 8vo, pp. 24, $2. New York, 1838

Like the Sybilline Books this pamphlet has become scarce, and every time it makes its appearance for sale will command a higher and higher price, not for any intrinsic merit the production possesses, but from the fact that it was written by the author whose name it bears. This Fourth of July Oration is the only known literary production that Mr. Forrest has been pleased to favor the public with. It might have been supposed that one so gifted would have been more copious in giving his views of times, things and men as they appeared to him both on and off the stage. No doubt the public expect an autobiography from him, and if they are not disappointed will find in said memoirs a series of pages not less interesting than Boswell's Life of Johnson, or the pleasing memoirs of Madame D'Arblay, Lady Montague, or Walpole's Letters, or the Diaries of old Burton, Evelyn, or Pepys, with this difference, that in place of delineating European characteristics he will draw American portraits of social life. At the time when his reputation for the personating strong and violent characters on the stage of the Bowery Theatre burst on the community like a drummond-light suddenly thrust into a dark alley in a murky night, I was connected with that institution, and of course had an opportunity of seeing him every night he performed. Mr. Forrest appeared to be possessed of the perfection of physical form, more especially conspicuous when arrayed in some peculiar costume, which tended to display it to the best advantage. He had a stentorian voice, and must have had lungs not less invulnerable than one of Homer's heroes whom he represents as having a throat of brass and adamantine lungs. He had a fine masculine face and prepossessing countenance, much resembling many of the notable Greeks and Romans whose portraits have come down to our time—a keen intellectual eye. His countenance at times assumed an air of hauteur which doubtless had become a habit either from personating characters of this stamp, or from a consciousness of his merited popularity. He left the impression on the beholder of one intoxicated with success and the repletion of human applause, feeling conscious that he had risen above all competition, and secured permanent reputation. Experience and riper years have doubtless modified and perhaps obliterated these early characteristics. He kept aloof from all around him, and condescended to no social intercourse with any one on the stage, and appeared to entertain a contempt for his audience. He was the subject for a long time of daily talk, more especially among the theatre play-goers. He made a visit to the land of his forefathers, where, during his sojourn, he appeared in the British metropolitan theatres and performed some of his favorite characters. We have it from the highest authority that there is a tide in the affairs of every man's life, which, if taken at the flood, leads on to fortune, but the candidate for eminence, distinction or fame, must take the advantage of the circumstance, that is to say, he must have all sails set, the steam up or both combined, as the case may be, and thus be in complete readiness for this fortunate juncture. Mr. Forrest had the perception as well as the capacity to improve this occasion, which but very few can do. At the commencement of his career he was fortunately favored by certain circumstances which materially aided his popularity and helped to spread his fame. First, the American people were in want of a hero to worship, so much so, that one from any of the professions or walks of life would have been acceptable.* The violent and vindictive partizan discussions which deluged the country during the Jackson administration had the effect to disgust all ranks of society, and prepared them to adopt a new favorite. Second, the Americans had never produced an actor who had added to the national reputation. Third, Mr. William Leggett, a man possessed of uncommon ability as a writer, more especially as a theatrical critic, took Mr. Forrest under his especial care, and by the aid of his genius through his paper made him favorably known throughout the country, and, as it were, opened the door to him wherever he went. After a lapse of thirty-five years I again witnessed Mr. Forrest personate two of his favorite characters, namely : Cardinal Richelieu, and Hamlet, Prince of Denmark. I must say as an actor he pleased me better in 1830 than he did in 1865. It would appear that these two renowned historical characters are not at all suited to the genius of Mr. Forrest, and his continuing to represent them may add to his treasury, but will by no means heighten his reputation. To personate the cunning, ambitious, and revengeful old priest who had held supreme power for a life time and about to be deprived of it, is not his part, and far less the solemn, high toned, philosophical character of Hamlet. These two characters are antipodes of each other, and require very different powers to set them forth to the life. The remarks made by Mr. Leggett respecting his reading and acting a few years after he commenced his career will apply with equal force at this time. " One of the most obvious faults in the manner of Mr. Forrest is a too slow and stately ennunciation, interrupted by frequent pauses — of such passages of the text as require to be spoken in a hurried, colloquial manner. In the unimpassioned parts of a character he is too apt to be declamatory, expressing himself with a regular rise and fall of voice, that strikes on the ear with the disagreeable effect of monotony. He abounds too much in gesture. This is a general fault of actors. In the exhibition of passion by his countenance Mr. Forrest usually keeps up the expression longer than is natural, thus producing a disagreeable or ludicrous effect." He has now lost that mercurial youthful appearance, which was then so conspicuous, and which doubtless aided in laying the foundation of his wide spread reputation ; he was then straight as an arrow and elastic as a circus rider, in short, he was the very beau-ideal of physical perfection. Now he bears the marks of decay, or rather, as it is said of grain just before the harvest time, he has a ripe appearance. When standing erect the knees are a little bent, besides a perceptible curve in the back and neck, and his whole frame manifesting a tendency to incipient corpulence. If he would consult his renown he would retire from the stage and never set foot upon it again During the nights of these performances he was favored with an overflowing house, the theatre was literally crammed from roof to foundation, but, as far as I could judge, by a very undiscriminating audience. They appeared to thunder out applause when there was no possible cause for it except the rauting noise of some performer, and kept mute and silent when they might have offered their approbation with propriety........................................WESTERN MEMORABILIA.

* Every nation, nay every individual, has its frail mutable golden-calf to whom it falls down and offers worship ; man by nature is prone to idolatry superinduced by a sense of his weakness and helplessness, and it may be said that his normal condition is eternal war with his race, in short, prone to do wrong. St. Paul gives the whole history of this his corrupt nature, thereby including every one else, in a single sentence : " When I would do good evil is present with me," and Socrates uttered a like sentiment, saying that his face indicated correctly that the natural bent of his mind was vicious. Till a more sublime and powerful religion than what is called natural overshadows and influences mankind, they must forever remain under the influence of this domineering nature.

Fox, George. The Life of, with Dissertations on his views concerning the Doctrines, Testimonies, and Discipline of the Christian Church, by Samuel M. Janney. 8vo, cloth, pp. 499, 82. Philadelphia, 1853

Francis, John W. Old New York ; or Reminiscences of the past Sixty Years, with a Memoir by Henry T. Tuckerman. Portrait and plate, royal 8vo, cloth, 815. New York, 1865.

Frankland. Sir Charles Henry, Baronet; or Boston in the Colonial Times, by Elias Nason, M.A. 8vo, clo., 82.50. Munsell, Albany, 1865

Fulton, Robert. A Treatise on the Improvement of Canal Navigation, exhibiting the numerous advantages to be derived from Small Canals. and boats of two to five tons burthen, with a description of the Machinery for facilitating conveyance by water, through the most mountainous countries, independent of Locks and Aqueducts; including Observations on the great importance of Water Communication, with Thoughts on, and Designs for Aqueducts and Bridges of Iron and Wood. Illustrated with seventeen Plates. 4to, pp. 144, very rare, in beautiful binding, 825. London, 1796

But few of Fulton's admirers are aware that he ever wrote such a book — few copies have reached this country, and perhaps but a few were printed. It is, consequently, a great rarity.

Gayarre, Charles. History of Louisiana under the French and Spanish Dominations. 3 vols., 8vo, cloth, 810.50. New York, 1854

## GENEALOGY.

Arthur, William. An Etymological Dictionary of Family and Christian Names, with an Essay on their derivation and import. 12mo, cloth. pp. 300, 81.50. New York. 1857

Bellows, Col. Benjamin. Historical Sketch of, Founder of Walpole. An address, on occasion of the gathering of his descendants to the consecration of his monument at Walpole. N. H., Oct. 11, 1854, by H. W. Bellows, with an appendix, containing an account of the family meeting. 8vo. pp. 125, 81.50. New York. 1855

Bowditch, N. I. Suffolk Surnames, 2d edition, enlarged. 8vo, pp. 398, 82.50. Boston. 1858

Brainerd. The Genealogy of the Brainerd Family in the United States, with numerous sketches of individuals, by Rev. D. D. Field. 8vo, cloth, portraits. pp. 303, 83. New York. 1857

Bridgman. John. An Historical and Topographical Sketch of Knole in Kent, with a brief Genealogy of the Sackville Family, with engravings. 8vo, pp. 164, 81.50. London, 1821

Cushmans. A Historical and Biographical Genealogy of the Cushmans, the descendants of Robert Cushman the Puritan, from the year 1617 to 1855. By H. W. Cushman. 8vo, cloth, pp. 665, 30 portraits, 85. Boston, 1855

Druce Family. A Genealogical Account of the, of Gorcing, in the county of Oxon, and those of kin to the children of George Druce, together with the different families of kin, their marriages. issue, &c. 4to, only 50 copies printed, large paper, 85 (fac-simile reprint). London, 1735

DUDLEY GENEALOGIES and Family Records. By Dean Dudley. 8vo, cloth, pp. 144, 82. Boston, 1848

GRACE FAMILY. Memoirs of the, by Shiffield Grace, Esq., F. R. S., full of Portraits, Coats of Arms, and Views. 8vo, 85. Private Print. London, 1823

GREENLEAF. A Genealogy of the Greenleaf Family, by Jonathan Greenleaf. 8vo, cloth, pp. 116, 82. Privately printed. N. York, 1854

GREVILLE FAMILY. An Historical and Genealogical Account of the noble family of Greville, to the time of Francis, the present Earl Brooke and Earl of Warwick, including the History and Succession of the several Earls of Warwick since the Norman Conquest, and some account of Warwick Castle. 8vo, pp. 108, plates. 82. London, 1766

HENRY, PHILIP. The Descendants of, Incumbent of Worthenbury, in the county of Flint, who was ejected therefrom by the act of uniformity in 1662. By Sarah Lawrence. 8vo, cloth, pp. 80. 82. London, 1844

HINMAM, ROYAL R. A Catalogue of the Names of the Early Puritan Settlers of the Colony of Connecticut, with the time of their arrival in the country and colony, their standing in society, place of residence, condition in life, where from, business, &c., as far as is found on record. 4 parts, 8vo, portrait, 812. Hartford, 1852

HOLGATE, JEROME B. American Genealogy; being a history of some of the early settlers of North America and their descendants, from their first emigration to the present time, with their intermarriages and collateral branches, &c., &c., pages from 80 to 105 missing. 2 parts, 4to, 810. Albany, 1848

HOLT. A Genealogical History of the Holt Family in the United States; more particularly the descendants of Nicholas Holt, of Newbury and Andover, Mass., 1634–1644, and of William Holt, of New Haven, Conn. By D. S. Durrie. 8vo, cloth, pp. 367, 85. Albany, 1864

JONES. Memorial of the late Hon. David S. Jones, with an Appendix, containing notices of the Jones Family, of Queen's county. Square 12mo, pp. 99 (some pages written on with ink), $1.50. N. Y., 1849

KENNEDY. Historical and Genealogical Account of the Principal Families of the Name of Kennedy, from an original manuscript, with notes and illustrations, &c. By Robert Pitcairn. 4to, pp. 227, 87.50. Edinburgh, 1830

KILBOURNE, PAYNE K. The History and Antiquities of the Name and Family of Kilbourn (in its varied orthography). 8vo, cloth, pp. 444, portraits and plates, 85. New Haven, 1865

LAWRENCE, JOHN. The Genealogy of the Family of Wisset, in Suffolk, England, and of Watertown and Groton, Massachusetts. 8vo, cloth, pp. 199, 85. Boston, 1857

MARMYUN. History of the Ancient Noble Family of Marmyun; their singular office of King's Champion, by the tenure of the Baronial Manor of Scrivelsby, in the county of Lincoln, &c., the whole collected at a great expense from the public records, with several curious engravings. 8vo, bds., pp. 218, 83. London, 1817

NEW ENGLAND (The). Historical and Genealogical Register, published quarterly, under the patronage of the New England Historic Genealogical Society. 10 vols., 8vo, cloth, portraits. $30. Bost., 1847, &c.

OTIS, RICHARD. A Genealogical Memoir of the family of. and collaterally of the families of Baker, Varney, Waldron, and many others. prepared and arranged by Horatio N. Otis, of N. York. 8vo. pp. 48. 81. Boston. 1851

RAYMOND, WILLIAM. Biographical Sketches of the Distinguished Men of Columbia county, including an account of the most important offices they have filled. 8vo, pp. 119. 82. Albany, 1851

RUDYERD, SIR BENJAMIN. Memoirs of, containing his Speeches and Poems; to which are added the letters of his great-great-grandson, Benjamin Rudyerd, Esq., and a Genealogy of the Rudyerd Family. Edited by J. A. Manning. 8vo, port., cl., pp. 410, 83. London. 1841

SALSBURGERS. The, and Their Descendants; being the history of a colony of German (Lutheran) protestants, who emigrated to Georgia in 1734. and settled at Ebenezer, 25 miles above Savannah, by Rev. P. A. Strobel. 12mo, cl., port. and plate, pp. 308, 83. Baltimore, 1855

SAVAGE, JAMES. A Genealogical Dictionary of the First Settlers of New England. showing three generations of those who came before May, 1692, on the basis of Farmer's Register. 4 vols., 8vo. cloth, $15. Boston, 1860

SIMS, R. An Index to the Pedigrees and Arms contained in the Heralds' Visitations, and other Genealogical Manuscripts in the British Museum. 8vo, cloth, pp. 336, 85. London, 1849

STEELE FAMILY. A Genealogical History of John and George Steele (settlers of Hartford. Conn.), 1635-6, and their Descendants, with an Appendix, containing genealogical information respecting other families of the name. By D. S. Durrie. 4to, large paper, pp. 155, 83. Albany, 1859

STILES, HENRY R. The History of Ancient Windsor, Conn., including East Windsor, South Windsor, and Ellington, prior to 1768, and Windsor, Bloomfield, and Windsor Locks, to the present time; also the Genealogies and Genealogical Notes of those families which settled within the limits of Ancient Windsor, Conn., prior to 1800, with Supplement. 2 vols., 8vo. cloth, 86. New York, 1859 and '63

TUFTON. Memorials of the Family of Tufton, Earls of Thanet, deduced from various sources of authentic information. 8vo. plate, boards, 82. Gravesend, 1800

WARD, ANDREW H. Family Register of the Inhabitants of the town of Shrewsbury. Mass., from its settlement in 1717 to 1829. and some of them to a later period. 8vo, port., pp. 294, 84. Boston, 1847

WATERTOWN. Family Memorials. Genealogies of the Families and Descendants of the Early Settlers of Watertown, Massachusetts, including Waltham and Weston. with the early history of the town, with illustrations, maps and notes. By Henry Bond, M.D. Two volumes in one, large thick 8vo, cloth. 86. Boston, 1855

WETMORE FAMILY. The, of America, and its collateral branches, with Genealogical, Biographical, and Historical Notices. By J. C. Wetmore. Royal 8vo, ½ morocco, pp. 680, 86. Munsell, Albany, 1861

GODMAN, JOHN D. American Natural History, 2d edition. 3 vols., 8vo, many plates, 86. Philadelphia. 1831

GORDON, THOMAS T. The History of New Jersey from its Discovery by Europeans to the adoption of the Federal Constitution, with a Gazetteer of the State of New Jersey, comprehending a general view of its Physical and Moral Condition, together with a Topographical and Statistical Account of its Counties, Towns, Villages, Canals, Rail roads, &c. 8vo, pp. 605, 83. Trenton, N. J., 1834

GRAHAME, JAMES. The History of the United States of North America, from the Plantation of the British Colonies till their Assumption of National Independence; second edition, enlarged and amended. 2 vols., 8vo, cloth, pp. 498 and 619, 83.50. Philadelphia, 1850

GREELEY, HORACE. Editor of the New York Tribune, Life of. By J. Parton. 12mo, pp. 446, plates, 81.50. New York, 1855

GREENOUGH, HORATIO. A Memorial of, consisting of a Memoir, Selections from his Writings and Tributes to his Genius. By Henry T. Tuckerman. 12mo, cloth, pp. 245, 81. New York. 1853

GRISWOLD, ALEXANDER VIETS. Me oir of the Life of, Bishop of the Protestant Episcopal Church in the Eastern Diocese, by John S. Stone, D.D., with an Appendix; to which are added a Sermon, Charge and Pastoral Letter of the late Bishop. 8vo, pp. 620, 82. Philadelphia, 1844

GURNEY, JOSEPH JOHN. Memoirs of, with selections from his Journal and Correspondence, edited by Joseph Bevan Braithwaite. 2 vols., 8vo, cloth, pp. 554 and 608, 83. Philadelphia, 1855

GROS, JOHN DANIEL. Natural Principles of Rectitude for the conduct of Man in all States and Situations of Life, demonstrated and explained in a systematic Treatise on Moral Philosophy. 8vo, pp. 456, 82. New York, 1795

This is believed to be the first treatise on Moral Philosophy written and published in America. The author was professor of that science in Columbia college, and the treatise was no doubt intended as a text book for the young men attending his class.

HALE, DAVID. Late Editor of the Journal of Commerce. Memoir of, with selections from his miscellaneous writings, by Joseph P. Thompson. 8vo, cloth, portrait, 81.25. New York, 1850

HALIBURTON, THOMAS C. An Historical and Statistical Account of Nova Scotia, illustrated by a map of the province and several engravings. 2 vols., 8vo, bds., 85. Halifax, 1829

HALL, JOHN, D.D. History of the Presbyterian Church in Trenton, N. J., from the first settlement of the Town. 12mo, cloth, pp. 460, wood cut, 81.50. New York, 1859

HALLOCK, GERRAD. History of the South Congregational Church, New Haven, from its origin in 1852 till Jan'y 1, 1865. 12mo, cloth, port. and plate, 81.50. New Haven, 1865

HAMILTON, SCHUYLER. The History of the National Flag of the United States of America, with 16 different flags beautifully colored. 12mo, cloth, pp. 115, 82. Phila., 1853

HAMMOND, JABEZ D. The History of Political Parties in the state of New York from the Ratification of the Federal Constitution of December, 1840. Fourth edition corrected and enlarged, to which are

4

added Notes by Gen. Root, with Portrait. 3 vols., 8vo, sheep, $6. Syracuse, 1849

HART. ADOLPHUS M. History of the Discovery of the Valley of the Mississippi. 12mo. pp. 155. 50 cts. St. Louis. 1852

HARVARD UNIVERSITY. Catalogus Senatus Academici. et eorum qui munera et officia gesserunt quique alicujus gradus laurea donati sunt, in Universitate Harvardiana Cantabrigiæ in Reipublica Massachusettensi. 8vo, interleaved, ½ calf. $2.50. Cantabrigiæ, 1842

HAWKS, FRANCIS L. A Narrative of Events connected with the Rise and Progress of the Protestant Episcopal Church in Virginia, with Journals of the Convention from 1785 to 1835, and Maryland. 2 vols., 8vo, pp. 618–523, $10. New York, 1836–39

HEAP. GWINN HARRIS. Central route to the Pacific, from the valley of Mississippi to California. Journal of the Expedition of E. F. Beale, Superintendent of Indian affairs in California, and Gwinn Harris Heap, from Missouri to California in 1853, with tinted illustrations. 8vo, cloth, pp. 131. $1. Philadelphia, 1854

HEARNE, SAMUEL. A Journey from Prince of Wales's Fort in Hudson's bay to the Northern ocean, undertaken by order of the Hudson's Bay Company. for the discovery of Copper Mines, a northwest passage, &c., in the years 1769, 1770, 1771 and 1772. 4to. ½ calf. pp. 500, maps and plates, neat, $8. London, 1795

HEMMENWAY. MOSES. A.M. A Vindication of the Power. Obligation and Encouragement of the Unregenerate to attend the means of Grace ; Against the exceptions of the Rev. Samuel Hopkins. in the second part of his reply to Rev. Mr. Mills, entitled. The true State and Character of the Unregenerate, stripped of all Misrepresentation and Disguise. 8vo. pp. 227, $3. Boston. 1772

HILDRETH. S. P. Pioneer History ; being an Account of the first Examinations of the Ohio Valley and the early Settlement of the Northwest Territory. chiefly from Original Manuscripts, containing the Papers of Col. George Morgan, those of Judge Barker, the Diaries of Joseph Buell and John Matthews, the Records of the Ohio Company, &c., &c., with maps and illustrations. 8vo. sheep, pp. 537, $3. Cincinnati, 1848

HILLIARD, HENRY W. Speeches and Addresses. 8vo, cloth, pp. 497, $2. New York, 1855

HINES. DAVID THOMAS. The Life, Adventures and Opinions of, of South Carolina. 12mo. pp. 195. $1.25. New York, 1840

HOLMS'S Account of the Province of New Sweden, called by the English, Pennsylvania ; adorned with maps and plates ; translated by Du Ponceau with notes. Extremely fine, clean copy. in bds., uncut, very rare. $5. Phila., 1834

HOUGH. FRANKLIN B. A History of Lewis county. in the state of New York, from the beginning of its settlement to the present time. 20 fine portraits. 8vo. pp. 323, $2.50. Albany. 1860

HUMPHREYS, DAVID. An Historical Account of the Incorporated Society for the Propagation of the Gospel in Foreign Parts, containing their Foundation, Proceedings and the Success of their Missionaries in the British Colonies, to the year 1728. 8vo, cloth, pp. 135, $1. London, 1730. reprinted 1852

HUNTER, JOHN D. Manners and Customs of several Indian Tribes located west of Mississippi, including some account of the Soil, Clime and Vegetable Productions, and the Indian Materia Medica. To which is prefixed the History of the Author's Life during a residence of several years among them. 8vo, bds., pp. 402, $2.25. Phil., 1823

ILLINOIS. United States of America. Documents relating to the organization of the Illinois Central Rail Road Company. Large map, 4to, pp. 146, $2.25. New York, 1851

INDIAN AFFAIRS. Annual Report of the Commissioners of the General Government from 1854 to 1864, both inclusive, with the exception of 1860. 10 vols., 8vo, cloth, $20. Washington, 1854-64
    " For authentic information respecting the present condition of the North American Indians these volumes may be consulted and relied upon, as the highest authority."

INDIAN GOOD BOOK, made by Eugene Vetromile, S. I. Indian Patriarch, for the benefit of the Penobscot, Passamaquoddy, St. John's, Micmac, and other tribes of the Abnaki Indians, Old Town Indian village, and Bangor. 3d ed., 12mo, pp. 586, illustrated, mor., gilt, 84. New York, 1858

INGERSOLL, CHARLES J. Historical Sketch of the second War between the United States of America and Great Britain, declared by act of Congress, the 18th of June, 1814, and concluded by peace, the 15th of February, 1815, embracing the events of 1814. 8vo, paper, pp. 317, $1. Philadelphia, 1849

IRVING, WASHINGTON. Irvingiana: A Memorial of. Small 4to, recumbent portrait and fac-simile letter, $1.25. New York, 1860

JAY. Treaty between the U. S. and Great Britain, with a letter from Jefferson on the subject, original ed., 12mo, uncut, $2. Phil, 1795

JEFFERSON, THOMAS. Notes of the State of Virginia. 8vo, calf, pp. 244, $3. Philadelphia, 1788

JEFFERSON, THOMAS. The Life of Late Ex-President of the United States arranged and compiled from original Documents, by T. P. H. Lyman. 8vo, pp. 111, portrait, $1.25. Philadelphia, 1826

JEFFERSON, THOMAS. Memoirs and Correspondence of, with a Fac-simile of the original draft of the Declaration of Independence. 4 vols., 8vo, bds., uncut, $6. Virginia, 1830

JEFFERSON, THOMAS. Works collected, arranged and annotated by H. A. Washington. 9 vols., 8vo, cloth, portrait and fac-similes. $20.
    New York, 1853

JEFFERSON, THOMAS, The Life of, by Samuel M. Smucker. 12mo, pp. 400, $1. Philadelphia, 1860

JEWITT, JOHN R. Narrative of the adventures and sufferings of, only survivor of the crew of the ship Boston, during a captivity of nearly 3 years among the Savages of Nootka Sound, with an account of the manners, mode of living, and religious opinions of the Natives. 18mo, sheep, plates, $1. Ithaca, N. Y., 1851

JOHNSON, SIR WILLIAM, BART. The Life and Times of, by Wm. L. Stone. 2 vols., 8vo, cloth. port., pp. 560-568, $5.50. Albany, 1865

KEMBLE, FRANCES ANN. Francis the First. A tragedy in five acts, with other poetical pieces; in which is included an original memoir and a full length portrait. 8vo, pp. 72, $1.50. New York, 1833

KEMBLE, FRANCES ANN.   The Star of Seville; a drama.   $1.50.
New York, 1837
KEMBLE, FRANCES ANN.   Poems by.   12mo, pp. 152, portrait. $1.
Philadelphia, 1844
KEMBLE, FRANCES ANN.   Poems, new edition.   12mo, pp. 309, $1.50.
Boston. 1859
KEMBLE, FRANCES ANN.   Journal of.   2 vols., 12mo, pp. 321–287, $2.
KEMBLE, FRANCES ANN.   Journal of a Residence on a Plantation in
Georgia in 1838–1839.   12mo, pp. 337, $1.25.    New York, 1863
KEMBLE. FRANCES ANN.   A year of Consolation.   2 vols., 12mo, pp.
136–171.   New York, 1847

FRANCES ANN KEMBLE.   Miss Fanny Kemble, afterwards Mrs. Butler, came to
America under the most favorable auspices. First, she was the scion of a family
which was well known, and which had shed lustre not only on the English
drama, but had added reputation to the British name. Second, she was accompanied by her father who had a well earned reputation for performing the
highest cast of character in genteel comedy. Third, she had personally earned
no mean reputation as a representative of the highest character in both tragedy
and comedy, besides being an authoress favorably known in both hemispheres,
and last she was young, prepossessing and by many would have been accounted
handsome, gifts which never fail to reach the hearts of the opposite sex. She
was courted and caressed by the gay, the fashionable, and the wealthy, even
to repletion (see her journal on this subject). Immense crowds flocked to
witness her performances; and on their return declared that she was matchless
as an actress and divine as a young and beautiful woman. Like all of her sex
who possess these qualities she soon attracted a host of rich and would be
wealthy admirers, and there is but little doubt but that she could designate any
one of them as her future companion. At length, however, a young and
wealthy planter as they were then called, but more properly speaking an extensive slave holder of Georgia, won the prize, and to the great delight of all
the young ladies north and disapointment of the young gentlemen, carried his
bride off to his negro stocked plantation, where she remained for one year and
perhaps a day. During that period becoming completely disgusted with what
she saw and heard respecting this peculiar domestic institution she left for a
more genial climate and associates, and where she would not be pained with the
every-day workings of slavery. She has preserved a journal of her impressions during her residence on this Georgia plantation in the year 1828, which
has been published for the enlightenment of those who believe in the divine
right of human slavery. Said journal is filled with a series of facts and observations touching that grim southern institution and its workings and as full of
truth as they are damning to that once boasted but now extinct power, which,
to ensure its own overthrow, committed suicide, but before performing this act
caused the death of one million of our brave soldiers and as a consequence
made two millions of helpless orphans, one million of weeping widows, and
plunged our government into a debt of over twenty-five hundred millions of
dollars, thereby imitating Sampson, who, if he was to fall, was determined to
pull the house down with him. Shortly after her arrival in America I recollect
witnessing her perform in the Park Theatre (a structure now no more). I have
forgot what the play was, but recollect she took the part of a young girl in the
middle ranks of English life; by the bye a class of young women remarkable
for loveliness of form and beautiful features in the extreme. On this occasion
she personated one of these lovely young maidens. Many and oft is the time
that I have seen the young female character represented on the stage both in
Europe and America, but never have I seen it in such admirable style as on
this occasion; every thing combined to render the personation as perfect as
could be, her form, her costume, her features, her age, the graceful disposition
of her hair, but above all her soft, mellow and feminine voice, aided by the
mimic variegated rural scenery which surrounded her lent matchless grace to
the parts. She excited the heart felt plaudits of the overcrowded audience.
Look upon this picture, and on this, more than fifteen years afterwards. In
the New York Tabernacle situated in Broadway and Worth street I heard the
same Fanny Kemble read one, or a portion of one of Shakespeare's plays to a
very crowded audience composed of intelligent citizens of both sexes. I confess her reading of Shakespeare had no more impression on me than water
thrown upon an oil cloth, but doubtless the fault was in me, not in the reader.

Her appearance now was totally altered ; in place of the young aerial, fascinating girl, she had assumed the proportions of a fat, overgrown, Irish cook, with full, round, high colored face, large bust and large arms. Such is the mutability in all earthly affairs....................................... WESTERN MEMORABILIA.

KEMBLE, FRANCES ANN. Mr. Butler's Statement, originally Prepared in aid of his Professional Counsel, including Letters from Mrs. Butler, now Frances Ann Kemble ; inserted full length portrait of Miss F. Kemble, with an autograph letter of P. Butler. 8vo, pp. 188, privately printed, $30. Sine Loco, Sine Anno.

This book, or rather the contents of it, presents a sad picture of domestic unhappiness — nay, positive connubial misery — apparently growing out of an uncongeniality of temper, diversity of disposition, and a total dissimilarity of tastes, arising from a different method of education and training in almost everything — religious, moral and domestic. If Mr. Butler has given a correct statement of what transpired between him and his wife, and there appears to be no doubt of the authenticity of the narrative, the only excuse that can be offered for Mrs. Butler's conduct is, that she was a monomaniac. It is another proof, among many, that he or she who has been accustomed to the stir and plaudits of a stage life, becomes totally unfit for a truly domestic husband or wife. Like all quarrels, national, local or domestic, both parties were more or less to blame...................................... WESTERN MEMORABILIA.

KEY, FRANCIS S. Poems of the late, author of the Star Spangled Banner, with an Introductory Letter by Chief Justice Taney. 12mo, cloth, pp. 208, $1. New York, 1857

LAMB, GEN. JOHN. Memoir of the Life and Times of, an Officer of the Revolution, who Commanded the Post at West Point at the Time of Arnold's Defection, and Correspondence with Washington, Clinton, Patrick Henry, and other Distinguished Men of his Time. By Isaac Q. Leake, with maps and a portrait. 8vo, cloth, pp. 451, $2. Albany, 1857

LATOUR, A. L. Historical Memoir of the War in West Florida and Louisiana in 1814-15, with an atlas. Translated by H. P. Nugent, Esq. 2 vols., 1 an atlas, 8vo, $5. Philadelphia, 1816

LEGARE, HUGH SWINTON. Writings of, consisting of a Diary of Brussells, and Journal of the Rhine, extracts from his Private and Diplomatic Correspondence, Orations and Speeches, and Contributions to the New York and Southern Review, preceded by a memoir of his life. 2 vols., 8vo, pp. 680-593, portrait, $10. Very scarce. Charleston, S. C., 1845

LEGGETT, WILLIAM. The Critic ; a Weekly Review of Literature, Fine Arts, and the Drama. Edited by William Leggett. Royal 8vo, pp. 509, $2. New York, 1828-29

LEGGETT, WILLIAM. The Plain Dealer. Small folio, $3. N. Y., 1856

LEGGETT, WILLIAM. Tales and Sketches of a Country Schoolmaster. 12mo, pp. 268, $1.50. New York, 1829

LEGGETT. WILLIAM. A Collection of the Political Writings of, selected and arranged, with a Preface. By Theodore Sedgwick. 2 vols., 12mo, pp. 312 and 336, $4. New York, 1840

LEGGETT, WILLIAM. Leisure Hours at Sea ; being a few Miscellaneous Poems, by a Midshipman of the United States Navy. 12mo, pp. 144, $5. Very rare. New York, 1825

William Leggett wrote two volumes of poems : the one unprocurable, and the other nearly as scarce. Of the one, the mechanical parts of the work were wholly done by his own hands ; that is to say, he was at once compositor, printer and binder ; which laborious task he achieved in 1820, or near that

date, while residing in the state of Illinois. This volume is without doubt the
first production of the muse that appeared in the then new state, and consequently a literary curiosity. He it was that brought Edwin Forrest prominently
and favorably before the public, through his literary periodical, entitled the
*Critic.* He was at one time coeditor of the *Evening Post* with Mr. Bryant, the
poet. During the copartnership they had a violent political controversy with
the editor of the *Courier and Enquirer,* wherein many epithets were used on
both sides, not very honorable to either party. The *Courier* dubbed them the
"chanting cherubs of the *Post,*" which name they retained for a long time
among other journalists throughout the country. He afterwards left the *Post*
and commenced a paper of his own, entitled the *Plain Dealer,* wherein the
peculiar characteristics of the editor were prominently displayed. This paper
lived for the short space of about one year, or a little more. After this he was
appointed by President Van Buren, American minister to Central America, but
immediately before the time appointed for his departure on this mission, he
was suddenly taken ill, and died at New Rochelle, in the vicinity of New York,
May 29, 1839................................................ Western Memorabilia.

Lincoln, Abraham. Political Debates between Hon. Abraham Lincoln
and Hon. Stephen A. Douglass, in the celebrated campaign of 1858,
in Illinois, including the preceding speeches of each, at Chicago,
Springfield, etc.; also, the two great speeches of Mr. Lincoln in Ohio,
in 1859, as carefully prepared by the reporters of each party. Royal
8vo, cloth, $1.25. Columbus, 1860

Lincoln, Abraham. A Tribute of Respect by the citizens of Troy, to
the Memory of. Royal 8vo, cloth, pp. 382, $3.50.
Munsell, Albany, 1865

Litchfield County. Centennial Celebration, held at Litchfield, Conn.,
13th and 14th of August, 1851. 8vo, cloth, $1. Hartford, 1851

Livingston, William. A Memoir of the Life of, Member of Congress
in 1774, 5 & 6, Governor of New Jersey from 1776 to 1790, &c.,
with extracts from his correspondence and notices of various members of his family, by Theodore Sedgwick, Jr. 8vo, portrait, pp.
456, $3.50. New York, 1833

Locke, Richard Adams. The Moon Hoax, or the discovery that the
Moon has a vast population of Human Beings. Illustrated with a
view of the Moon as seen by Lord Ross's Telescope. 8vo, pp. 63,
$1. New York, 1859

Log College. Biographical Sketches of the Founders and principal
Alumni of Log College, collected by A. Alexander. 12mo, pp, 369,
$1. Princeton, N. J., 1845
The biographies given in this volume are, Wm. Tennent, Gilbert Tennent,
John Tennent, Wm. Tennent, Jr., Samuel Blair, John Blair, Samuel Finlay,
D.D., Wm. Robinson, John Rowland and Charles Beatty.

Lossing, B. J. The National History of the United States, from the
period of the union of the colonies against the French, to the inauguration of Washington, together with historical sketches of the Continental Presidents, &c. Also the Lives of the Presidents, with the
acts of their administrations. To which is added valuable historical
and statistical documents, by Edwin Williams. Illustrated with
numerous portraits and views. 2vols., royal 8vo, cloth, pp. 696–
676, $6. New York, 1855

Louis XVII. An Abridged Account of the Misfortunes of the Dauphin,
followed by some Documents in support of the facts related by the
Prince, with a supplement. Translated from the French, by the
Hon. and Rev. C. G. Percival. 8vo, pp. 714, $2. London, 1838

Louis XVII. His Life and Sufferings, his Death; the Captivity of the

Royal Family in the Temple, by Dr. Beauchesne. Translated and edited by W. Hazlet. Numerous Fac-similes. 2 vols., 12mo, $3.50.

London, 1853

ELEAZER WILLIAMS, the reputed Louis the XVII. The story of his life is this, namely : He was the son of Maria Antoinette, by Louis the XVI, and shortly after his birth was committed to the care of some unknown person who either carried or had him sent to North America, where he was consign ed to a certain tribe of Indians residing in the western part of New York, who adopt ed him as a son, and by whom he was brought up to their wild habits and customs. By some means or other he obtained a good education, and after due prepara- tion was ordained by Bishop Hobart, an Episcopal clergyman, in 1826, and as such, spent the best part of his life as a missionary among the Indians. Many newspaper articles, pamphlets, and even books have been written pro and con, discussing this remarkable controversy of his claims to the French Dauphinship. On a certain occasion I took the liberty of asking him what were his own views on this subject. In reply, he said that ambition, worldly pride, vanity, and notoriety would seem to prompt his carnal mind to adopt the views, that he was the actual heir to the French throne, but again said he, Christian humility, and a consciousness of my position forbids me to entertain such worldly and ambi- tious views, I therefore have left the whole subject to others who feel an interest in such discussions, to make of it what they may. He appeared to me to have a striking resemblance to that most unfortunate and by far the best of all French monarch Louis XVI, as he is represented to us by the engraved portraits which have come down to our time, large, massy, full face, acquiline nose, dark eye, swarthy complexion, heavy, corpulent frame, and he spoke in a slow, solemn tone; in short, his venerable countenance left the impression on the beholder of extreme benevolence and good will to all men. I took him to be a Christian man, imbued with heart-felt piety which controlled his every emotion, and was carried into all the ramifications of life. I think none could be more thoroughly devout, not even Pascal, Baxter, or Boston, who all have the reputation of having come nearest the perfect Christian.................... WESTERN MEMORABILIA.

LOUISIANA. Historical Collections of, embracing many rare and valuable documents, relating to the Natural, Civil and Political History of the State. Edited by B. F. French. 8vo, 5 vols., $12.50.

New York, 1846–52

MABLY, ABBE DE. Remarks concerning the Government and the Laws of the U. S. of America, in four letters addressed to Mr. Adams, with notes by the Translator. 8vo, pp. 280, $1.25. Dublin, 1785

MACKENZIE, WILLIAM L. The Life and Times of Martin Van Buren, Benjamin F. Butler, and Jessie Hoyt, with the correspondence of their friends, families and pupils, with brief notices, sketches and anecdotes. 2 vols., 8vo, paper cover, $2. New York, 1846

The publication of these volumes gave so much offence to the parties con- cerned that they were prohibited from being sold at the time of publication by injunction. The book made some uncomfortable revelations touching the ac- tions and conduct of many of the leading Democratic politicians who figured largely during General Jackson's times. The compiler was charged with ob- taining the documents which form the text of these volumes surreptitiously by having purloined them from the Archives of the Custom House of New York, where he was employed then as a clerk................ WESTERN MEMORABILIA.

MAN'S WHOLE DUTY: or the Rule of a Christian's Life and Conversa- tion, containing plain and short directions for the performance of the several duties thereof. 18mo, pp. 84, 83. Boston, 1718

MANUAL for the use of the Legislature of the State of New York, from the first, 1840 to 1863, wants 1849–50. 21 vols., $15.

Albany, 1840–63

MARTIN, JOSEPH AND W. H. BROCKENBROUGH. A Comprehensive De- scription of Virginia, and the District of Columbia ; containing a copious collection of Geographical, Statistical, Political, Commercial, Religous, Moral and Miscellaneous Information, chiefly from original sources, by J. M. To which is added a History of Virginia, from its first settlement to the year 1724, with an abstract of the principal events from that period to the Independence of Virginia, by W. H. B. 8vo, $3. Richmond, Va., N. D.

MARYLAND. Gazetter of the State of, compiled from the seventh census of U. S. and other official documents. To which is added a general account of the District of Columbia, by R. S. Fisher, M.D. 8vo, cloth, map, $1.25. N. York and Balt., 1852

MASERES. F. An account of the Proceedings of the British and other Protestant Inhabitants of the Province of Quebec, in North America, in order to obtain an House of Assembly in that province, pp. 294. Additional papers concerning the Province of Quebec, being an appendix to the above. pp. 510. 2 vols., 8vo, calf, $6.
London, 1775-6

MASON AND DIXON'S LINE. The History of, contained in an address by John H. B. Latrobe of Maryland, before the Historical Society of Pennsylvania, Nov. 8, 1854. 8vo, pp. 52, $1.50. Phila., 1855

MEADE, BISHOP. Old Churches. Ministers and Families of Virginia. 2 vols., 8vo, cloth, numerous plates, $5. Phila., 1861

METEOROLOGICAL REGISTER. Army, for twelve years, from 1843 to 1854, inclusive, compiled from observations made by the officers of the medical department of the Army, at the military posts of the U. S. prepared under the direction of Gen. Thomas Lawson, Surgeon General U. S. A. Published by authority of Hon. Jefferson Davis, Secretary of War. 4to, ½ mor., pp. 777. $5. Washington, 1855

METHODIST EPISCOPAL CHURCH. Journal of the General Conference of the, held in Buffalo, N. Y., 1860. Edited by William L. Harris, D.D. 8vo, mor., pp. 480, $2. New York, 1860

MILLER, STEPHEN F. The Bench and Bar of Georgia; Memoirs and Sketches, with an appendix, containing a court roll from 1790 to 1857, etc. 2 vols., 8vo, $8. Philadelphia, 1858

MILNOR, JAMES. D.D. Late Rector of St. George's church, New York, A memoir of the Life of, by the Rev. John S. Stone. 8vo, cloth, pp. 646, portrait and plate. $1.50. New York, 1848

MINER, CHARLES. History of Wyoming, in a series of letters to his son William Penn Miner, Esq. Illustrated. 8vo, cloth. pp. 607, map, $5. Philadelphia, 1845

MIRABEAU, COMTE DE. Considerations sur l'ordre de Cincinnatus, ou Imitation d'un pamphlet Anglo-American. Suivies de plusieurs Pieces relatives à cette Institution. D'un Lettre signée du General Washington, accompagnee de remarques par l'Auteur François, &c. 8vo, pp. 397, $5. Londres, 1784

MINOT, GEORGE RICHARDS. Continuation of the History of the Province of Massachusetts bay, from the the year 1748, with an introductory sketch of events from its original settlement. 2 vols. bound in 1, 8vo, cloth, pp. 526, $3. Boston, 1798

MOORE, JACOB BAILEY. Lives of the Governors of New Plymouth and Massachusetts bay, from the landing of the Pilgrims at Plymouth in 1620, to the union of the two colonies in 1692. 8vo, cloth, pp. 439, $1.50. Boston, 1851

MORTON, SAMUEL GEORGE. Crania Americana; or a Comparative view of the *Skulls of various Aboriginal Nations of North and South America*. To which is prefixed an Essay on the Varieties of the Human Species. Illustrated by seventy-eight plates and a colored map. Folio, pp. 297. $50. Very scarce. Philadelphia, 1829

MULFORD, ISAAC S. A Civil and Political History of New Jersey, embracing a Compendious History of the State from its Early Discovery and Settlement by Europeans, brought down to the present time. 8vo, cloth, pp. 500, $2. Philadelphia, 1851

MUNSELL, JOEL. Collections on the History of Albany, from its Discovery to the present time, with Notices of its Public Institutions, and Biographical sketches of citizens deceased, vol. 1. Royal 8vo, cloth, pp. 585, portraits and plates. Munsell. $10. Albany, 1865

NATIONAL PREACHER (The), or Original Monthly Sermons from Living Ministers. Edited by Austin Dickinson, M.A., New York, from vol. 1, 1826, to vol. 36, 1862. In 16 vols., 8vo, half bound. $24.
New York, 1826-62

NATIONAL PORTRAIT GALLERY (The), of Distinguished Americans. Conducted by James B. Longacre, Phil., and James Herring, New York. Under the Superintendence of the American Academy of the Fine Arts. 4 vols., 8vo, full morocco, gilt, containing 144 steel portraits, $25. Philadelphia. 1837

NAVAL CHRONICLE. The United States Naval Chronicle, by Charles W. Goldsborough. 8vo, $1.50. Washington, 1824

NEVIN. ALFRED. Churches of the Valley: or an Historical Sketch of the Old Presbyterian Congregations of Cumberland and Franklin counties in Pennsylvania. 12mo, cloth, pp. 338, $1.25.
Philadelphia, 1852

NEW HAMPSHIRE AND VERMONT. Gathered Sketches from the Early History of. Containing vivid and interesting accounts of a great variety of the adventures of our forefathers, and of other incidents of olden time. Edited by Francis Chase, M.A. 12mo, plates, $1.25. Claremont. N. H., 1856

NEW YORK CITY. Corporation Manuals, from the commencement in 1841 to 1865. With numerous fac-similies, maps, view and plates. 24 vols., 24mo, 18mo, and 12mo. Compiled by David Valentine.
New York, 1841-65

This series of books (The New York Corporation Manuals) has become an important item in the antiquarian, historical, biographical and literary annals of the city of New York. To those desiring information about the city, or who may be writing on the subject, these books will be found indispensable repositories of information. Mr. Valentine deserves well, and more than well, of the Community, and of posterity which will come after him, for having been such a faithful and judicious gleaner of these scattered historic fragments and antiquarian facts, and giving them a shape which will command respect, as well as to secure them a permanency. The collection of fac-similes and maps alone, to say nothing of the engraved views, are of great intrinsic value, and possess a charming interest to all who love to contemplate past transactions.
WESTERN MEMORABILIA.

NEW YORK MIRROR, The, and Ladies' Literary Gazette; being a Repository of Miscellaneous Literary productions in Prose and Verse. Edited by Samuel Woodworth, N. P. Willis, and George P. Morris. A complete set, in parts, with numerous engravings. 20 vols., 4to, $100. New York, 1823-42

This periodical commenced being published August 2, 1823, and terminated with the twentieth volume, December 24, 1842. During its career almost every writer in America, whether celebrated or obscure, was a contributor to the columns of the *Mirror*, and on this account it still possesses unusual interest. The following are the names of some of the contributors: N. P. Willis, Gulian C. Verplank, Fanny Kemble, William Leggett, Willis Gaylord Clark, Prosper M. Wetmore, James K. Paulding, Samuel Woodworth, William H. Harrison, John G. Whittier, Matthew Carey, John Howard Payne, John W. Francis, Grenville Mellen, Samuel L. Knapp. F. W. Thomas, Washington Irving, Epes Sargent, Mrs. Norton, Miss Landon, Rufus Dawes, James Sheridan Knowles, G. P. R. James, John Inman, Charles Fenno Hoffman, Jean Paul, Robert C. Sands, Theodore S. Fay, William Fox, L. H. Sigourney, James Nack, John Neal, James Lawson, Solomon Brown, Grant Thorburn, Richard Adams Locke, George D. Prentice, Tyrone Power, Mrs. Welby, Lydia Jane Pearson, James Fenimore Cooper, J. Augustus Shea, Harriet Beecher Stowe, George P. Morris, Thomas Dunn English, Cornelius Matthews, Robert M. Baird, &c., &c.

NEW YORK ALMANACS of HUGH GAINE, and others, from 1781 to 1857, both inclusive, wanting 1790 – 1804 – 19 – 26 – 27 – 29 – 31 – 33 – 34 – 35 – 36 – 37 – 38 – 1843 – 44 – and 1848. In all 60 numbers. $30.  New York, 1781 – 1857

NEW YORK. The Natural History of the State of New York, with an astonishing profusion of plates — some colored; and a lengthy Introduction by the Hon. William H. Seward. 19 vols., 4to, map, $110.  Albany, 1842 – 55

NEW YORK DIRECTORY, The, containing the names of citizens, their occupations and places of abode; the Members of Congress, from what State and where residing; a valuable and well calculated Almanac. With a plan of the city of New York, as it then appeared, &c., &c. Compiled by David Franks. 18mo, pp. 82, 82.

New York, 1786. Reprinted, 1851

The above is a fac-simile reprint of the first New York City Directory. It has now become very interesting, as nothing can show better at one glance, the vast improvements in the city, than the comparing of this directory with the one last published. The first like a new born infant, the second like a great overgrown giant; the inhabitants then numbered about 4,000, now about 800,000; and this all in the space of seventy years. The limit of the buildings of the city then was in Broadway at the head of Pearl street, now the high bridge that conveys the Croton water over the Harlem river, that supplies the city with water, a distance of eleven miles from Castle Garden.

NEW YORK DIRECTORIES. From 1786 to 1866, inclusive. 80 vols., 12mo and 8vo, $350.00.  New York, 1786 – 1866

There can be no better chronological step-ladder for presenting in a clear light the gradual growth or decline of a city than a consecutive series of its directories, giving annually the number of houses with the names of the respective householders thereof, public institutions and private enterprises, &c. Here are facts without fiction or coloring; a solid base for correct estimate; In short, a reliable reference book not to be doubted. It must be remembered that statistics is the corner stone of history; without them history would degenerate into romance and unmeaning fiction. A series of New York Directories form a perfect miniature of the rise and progress of the American Metropolis.

NEW YORK. Documents relative to the Colonial History of the State of New York; procured in Holland, England and France, by John Romeyn Brodhead, Esq. Edited by E. B. O'Callahan, M.D. LL.D. 10 vols., 4to, cloth, maps and portraits, $20.  Albany, 1856 – 58

NEW YORK. Journal of the Convention of the State of New York: began and held at the city of Albany, on the 13th day of October, 1801. 4to, unbound, uncut, pp. 42, $5.  Albany, 1801

NILES, H. Principles and Acts of the Revolution in America: or an attempt to collect and preserve some of the Speeches, Orations and Proceedings, with sketches and remarks on Men and Things, and other fugitive or neglected pieces, &c., &c. Royal 8vo, pp. 503, $5. Baltimore, 1822

NORTH AMERICAN REVIEW. From the Commencement, less the following: Nos. 14–15–16 old series, and 119–120–121–159–161–164–166–167–184 and 186 new series. Bound and in boards, the remainder in parts. $125.00. Boston, 1815–60
The chief contributors to the *North American Review* were the following: Edward Everett, George Bancroft, Caleb Cushing, J. Blunt, Dr. D. Ward, Jared Sparks, B. Emmerson, Professor Hedge, W. H. Prescott, William Philips, Alexander H. Everett, Dr. Byllow, S. Gilman, T. Parsons, A. Hall, Henry Wheaton, W. Peabody, O. Dewey, S. Sewell, W. Felton, A. Richie, E. Brooks, J. Ware, T. Metcalf, T. Gray, W. H. Gardner, C. G. Cogswell, M. Stuart, —— Lamson, Lewis Cass, W. C. Channing, H. Ware, Professor Hitchcock, Professor Ripley, H. Schoolcraft, —— Greenwood, &c., &c.

NORTH AMERICAN REVIEW. From vol. X, vol. 1, new series, 1821, to vol. 50,–1840, wants all after vol. 30, except vols. 46–47–48–49 and 50. 36 vols., 8vo, $36. Boston, 1821–40

ORATIONS. An Oration on the 4th of July, 1799, at New Haven, by David Daggett, pp. 28. N. H., 1799. Oration spoken at Hartford, July 4, 1799, by William Brown, pp. 23. Hartford, 1799. Oration at Hartford, May 8, 1794, by Theodore Dwight, pp. 24. Hartford, 1794. Oration at Hartford, July 4, 1798, by Theodore Dwight, pp. 31. Hartford, 1798. Oration at New Haven, July 7, 1801, by Theodore Dwight, pp. 43. Hartford, 1801. A Poem sacred to the memory of *George Washington.* Adapted to the 22d of February, 1800, by Richard Alsop, pp. 23. Hartford, 1800. Oration at Wallingford, March 11, 1801, for the election of Thomas Jefferson for President, and of Aaron Burr for Vice-President of the United States, by Abraham Bishop, pp. 111. New Haven, 1801. One vol., 8vo, $4.
Hartford, &c., V. D.

OWEN, DAVID DALE. Report of a Geological Survey of Wisconsin, Iowa and Minnesota; and incidentally, of a portion of Nebraska Territory. Made under instructions from the United States Treasury Department. 4to, pp. 639, cloth, maps and plates. $6.
Phila., 1852
This magnificent work is adorned with 72 wood engravings, giving views of the most remarkable places and objects in the countries described. A large geological map of the whole district, elaborately colored, embracing Wisconsin, Iowa and Minnesota, together with portions of Missouri and Illinois. A map of Wisconsin and Minnesota, showing the extension of the rock formations concealed under the drift. 12 engravings on steel and 9 on stone, showing organic remains and other geological curiosities of this lately explored country.

OWEN, ROBERT DALE. Hints on Public Architecture, containing among other illustrations views and plans of the Smithsonian Institution; together with an Appendix relative to building materials, prepared on behalf of the building committee of the Smithsonian Institution. 4to, pp. 129, unbound, $5. New York, 1848

PACIFIC RAIL ROAD. Reports of Explorations and Surveys, to ascertain the most practicable and economical route for a rail road from the Mississippi to the Pacific Ocean, made under the direction of the Secretary of War, in 1853 and 4. 13 vols., 4to, half bound, maps and colored plates. Washington, 1855 &c.

It may be said that as a general thing the titles of books announce much
more than their contents will warrant, but the Pacific Rail Road Survey Reports
is an exception to this rule, for in place of a simple Engineer's report, it is in
reality a complete body of natural history of a vast region of heretofore unex-
plored country. The plates representing the objects of natural history are ex-
quisitely executed and life like colored. It cost the government of the United
States over one million of dollars. To the Student of natural history the pe-.
rusal of these volumes will prove a mental feast, far beyond anything that he
has ever ,studied heretofore. ......................WESTERN MEMORABILIA.

PANAMA MASSACRE, (The), a Collection of the Principal Evidence and
other Documents, including the Report of Amos B. Corwine, Esq.,
U. S. Commissioner; the Official Statement of the Governor and the
Depositions taken before the Authorities, relative to the Massacre of
American Citizens at the Panama Rail-road Station, on the 15th of
April, 1856. Printed for private circulation. Royal 8vo, unbound,
uncut, pp. 69, $1. Panama, 1857

PARISH WILL CASE, A Report of. 3 vols., royal 8vo, pp. 778 – 799 –
794, $10. New York, 1857

PAULDING, I. Affairs and Men of New Amsterdam in the Time of
Governor Peter Stuyvesant. Compiled from Dutch manuscript records of the period. 12mo, pp. 163, $3. New York, 1843

PENHALLOW, SAMUEL. The History of the Wars of New England
with the Eastern Indians, or a Narrative of their continued Perfidy
and Cruelty, from the 10th of August 1703, to the Peace Renewed,
13th day of July 1713, and from the 25th of July, 1722, to their
Submission, 15th of December, 1725. 4to, cloth, pp. 129, $3.
Cincinnati, 1859

PENN, WILLIAM. A Collection of the Works of, to which is prefixed
a Journal of his Life, with many Original Letters and Papers not
before published. 2 vols., folio, $12. London, 1726

PENN, WILLIAM. A Brief Account of the Rise and Progress of the
People called Quakers, in which their Fundamental Principles, Doctrine, Worship, Ministry and Discipline, are plainly declared, &c.
12mo, pp. 95, $1. Philadelphia, 1816

PERKINS, JAMES H. Annals of the West. Embracing a Concise Account of Principal Events, which have occurred in the Western
States and Territories, from the Discovery of the Mississippi Valley,
to the year 1850. Compiled from the most authentic sources, for
the Projector. First edition, by James H. Perkins; second edition,
revised and enlarged, by James M. Peck. 8vo, pp. 808, $4.
St. Louis, 1850

PETERSON. EDWARD. History of Rhode Island. Illustrated. 8vo,
cloth, pp. 370, $2. New York, 1853

PIDGEON, WILLIAM. Traditions of De-Coo-Dah, and Antiquarian Re-
searches ; comprising Extensive Explorations, Surveys and Excava-
tions of the Wonderful and Mysterious Earthen Remains of the
Mound Builders in America; the Traditions of the last Prophet of
the Elk Nation relative to their Origin and Use ; and the Evidences
of an Ancient Population more numerous than the Present Abori-
gines. Embellished with 70 engravings, descriptive of 120 vary-
ing relative arrangements, forms of earthen effigies, antique sculpture, &c. 8vo, pp. 334, $2. New York, 1858

PINKERTON, JOHN. A General Collection of the Best and most Interesting Voyages and Travels in various parts of America, viz: vol. 1, Dampier's Account of the Philippines, Observations on the Philippine Islands, and the Isle of France, from the French of M. De Guignes. Beeckman's Voyage to Borneo. Account of Java, and Batavia, from the Voyages of Stavorinus. Account of Celebes, Amboyna, &c. Pigafetta's Voyage around the World. Extract from the Treatise on Navigation of A. Pigafetta. Australasia, from the work of President De Brosses. Pelsart's Voyage to Australasia. Tasman's Voyage for the Discovery of Southern Countries. Dampier's Account of New Holland. Abstract of Capt. Cook's First Voyage, do. 2d and last Voyage for the Discovery of Southern Lands, from the French of M. Perron. Vol. 2. Colon's Discovery of the West Indies. Discoveries made by the English in America, from the Reign of Henry VII. to the Close of that of Queen Elizabeth. Frobisher's First Voyage in Search of the North West Passage to China, made in 1576. Frobisher's Second Voyage, made for the Discovery of the North West Passage, made in 1577, with a Description of the Country and People. Frobisher's third Voyage for the Discovery of the North West Passage, made in 1578. Discovery of and Voyages to Virginia. Cartier's Discovery of the Island of New France. Vol. 3, Smith's History of Virginia, New England, and the Summer Isles. Lahontan's Travels in Canada. Memoirs of North America. Kalm's Travels in North America. Burnaby's Travels through the Middle Settlements in North America, in 1759, and 1760. Vol. 4. Betagh's Account of Peru. Ovalle's Historical Relation of Chili. Condamine's Travels in South America. Bouguer's Voyage to Peru. Ulloa's Voyage to South America. Nieuhoff's Voyages and Travels into Brazil. 4 vols., 4to. boards, uncut, illustrated. $20.                                         London, 1818

POOLE, FRED. An index to Periodical Literature. royal one half morocco gilt edged, 8vo, pp. 521, 86.                         New York, 1853
  The above is a very full index to all subjects treated of in not less than seventy-three of the most popular periodicals published in Great Britain and the United States during the present century. It will be found an immense saving labor machine to any person having cause to use these store-houses of intellectual riches.

PRO-SLAVERY ARGUMENT, THE, as maintained by the most distinguished Writers of the Southern States. Containing the Several Essays on the subject of Chancellor Harper, Governor Hammond, Dr. Simms, and Professor Dew. 12mo, cloth, pp. 490, $1.50.
                                                    Charleston, 1852

PUTNAM, ISRAEL, The Veil Removed, or Reflections on David Humphrey's Essay on the Life of. Also Notices of Oliver W. B Peabody's Life of the same; S. Swift's Sketch of the Bunker Hill Battle, &c., &c. By John Fellows. 12mo, cloth, pp. 231. $1.
                                                    New York, 1843

RAMSAY, DAVID. The History of South Carolina, from the First Settlement in 1670, to 1808. 2 vols., 8vo, maps, half calf, neat, $16.
                                                    Charleston, 1809

RAMSEY, S. G. M. The Annals of Tennessee, to the End of the Eighteenth Century. Comprising its Settlement as the Watauga Association, from 1769, to 1777; a Part of North Carolina, from 1777 to 1784; The State of Franklin, from 1784, to 1788 ; a Part of North Carolina, from 1788, to 1790 ; the Territory of the United States, South of the Ohio, from 1790 to 1796; the State of Tennessee, from 1796 to 1800. Map. 8vo, cloth, pp. 748, 84.　　　Philadelphia, 1853

REESE, DAVID M.　Humbugs of New York ; being a Remonstrance against Popular Delusion, whether in Science, Philosophy or Religion, 12mo. pp. 273, $1.50.　　　New York, 1838

REES, JAMES.　The Dramatic Authors of America. 12mo, pp. 144, $1.
　　　Philadelphia, 1845
A work showing a considerable amount of bibliographical industry. Here is a little book giving a catalogue of one hundred and eleven American Dramatic authors, with a list of their respective plays, occasional short biographical sketches, notices of some of the American Theatres throughout the country and a meagre chronology of the American Theatre. Although the author has aimed at alphabetical arrangement, his book is quite defective in this respect, as well as in others, having neither chapters, headings, prominent catch words, chronological arrangement, contents nor index ; besides he has quite defaced his book by occasionally introducing parts of scenes of certain plays which has much incumbered his performance, without adding interest or value to it. Notwithstanding all this, the author deserves great credit for this performance, inasmuch as it is the first and only one of the kind (so far as I can learn), that has appeared in the country. It will be an excellent nucleus for a more extended and better arranged treatise on the same subject.
　　　WESTERN MEMORABILIA.

RICHMOND IN BY GONE DAYS.　By an old Citizen, 12mo, cloth, $1.50.
　　　Richmond, 1856

RIGGS, S. R.　Grammar and Dictionary of the Dakotah Language, collected by the members of the Dakotah Mission, 4to, pp. 333, $6.
　　　Washington, 1852

RITTER, ABRAHAM.　History of the Moravian Church in Philadelphia, from its Foundation in 1742 to the Present Time ; Comprising Notices, Defensive of its Founder and Patron, Count N. L. Von Zinzendorff together with an Appendix. 8vo., cloth, portraits and plates, $2.
　　　Philadelphia, 1857

RUSSELL. LORD JOHN.　(Fourth Duke of Bedford), Correspondence of, edited by Lord John Russell. 3 vols., 8vo, cloth, $6.50.
　　　London, 1846
These volumes are of great value to the student of American Colonial History, especially immediately before the breaking out of the Revolution. Mr. Bancroft speaks in the highest terms of this book.

RUSSELL, WILLIAM HOWARD.　My Diary, North and South. 12mo, cloth, $1.　　　Boston, 1863

SAFFELL, W. T. R.　Records of the Revolutionary War, containing the Military and Financial Correspondence of Distinguished Officers, names of the Officers and Privates of Regiments, Companies, and Corps, with the Dates of their Commissions, and Enlistments. General Orders of Washington, Lee, and Greene, at Germantown and Valley Forge ; with a List of Distinguished Prisoners of War.. &c. &c. 12mo, pp. 554, cloth, $2　　　Philadelphia, 1860

SANDS, ROBERT C.　Writings in Prose and Verse, viz : Yomaden ; or the Wars of King Philip, a Poem with Historical Notes. Garden of Venus. a Poem. History of Cortez. Edited by G. C. Verplanck. 2 vol., 8vo, port, $3.　　　New York, 1834
Sands gave promise to be a great ornament to American Literature, but the grim conqueror put a stop to his promising career.

SARGENT, WINTHROP. The History of an Expedition against Fort Du Quesne, in 1755, under Major-General Edward Braddock. Edited from the original manuscripts, eleven illustrations. 8vo, pp. 423, $3.25
Philadelphia, 1855

SCHUYLER, PHILIP, The Life and Times of, by Benson J. Lossing. 2 portraits, 8vo, cloth, vol. 1. (all published so far), $1.50. N.Y., 1860

SELECT LETTERS on the Trade and Government of America, and the Principles of Law and Policy, Applied to the American Colonies. Written by Governor Bernard, at Boston,in the years 1763, 4, 5, 6, 7, and 8. Now first published, to which are added the Petition of the Assembly of Massachusetts Bay against the Governor, his Answer thereto, and the Order of the King in Council thereon. 8vo, unbound, pp. 137, $2.                                    London, 1774

SCHOOLCRAFT, HENRY R. Summary Narrative of an Exploratory Expedition to the Sources of the Mississippi River, in 1820, Resumed and Completed by the Discovery of its Origin in Itasca Lake, in 1832, by authority of the United States, &c., &c. 8vo, cloth, pp. 596, map, $2.50.                                           Philadelphia, 1855

SEWALL, J. M. Miscellaneous Poems, with Specimens from the Author's Manuscript Version of the Poems of Ossian. 12mo, pp. 304, $5.
Portsmouth, N. H.. 1801
The above is one of the scarcest of all the produtions of the early American Poets. On enquiring at several of the great libraries in Boston, Cambridge, Providence, New York and Philadelphia, not one of them was found to possess a copy of this book. Sewell was the author of the oft quoted, or rather mis-quoted couplet :
    " No pent up Utica contracts your pow'rs,
     But the whole boundless Continent is yours."

SEWARD, WILLIAM H., The Works of, edited by George E. Baker. 3 vols., 8vo, cloth, port, $15.                                    New York, 1853

SEYBERT, ADAM. Statistical Annals ; Embracing View of the Population, Commerce, Navigation, Fisheries, Public Lands, Post Offices, Revenues, Mint, Military and Naval Establishments. &c., &c.. of the United States of America; founded on Official Documents. 4to, pp. 803, published at $15 — 3.                                    Philadelphia, 1818

SHELDON's History of Michigan, from the First Settlement. 8vo, portraits, $1.50.                                              New York, 1856

SILLIMAN, BENJAMIN. The American Journal of Science and Art, from vol. 30, 1836, to vol. 39, 1840, both included, wanting vol. 38. 9 vols., 8vo, half calf, $11.25.              New Haven, 1836 – 40

SIMES, THOMAS. A new Military, Historical and Explanatory Dictionary, pp. 138, Philadelphia, 1776. General Wolfe's Instructions to Young Officers, also his Orders for a Battalion and an Army, &c , pp. 143, Philadelphia, 1778. Extract from a Military Essay, containing Reflections on the Raising, Arming, Clothing and Discipline of the British Infantry and Cavalry ; by C. Dalrymple, pp. 31, Philadelphia, 1776. The Manual Exercise, as ordered by His Majesty, in the year 1764, pp. 35, Philadelphia, 1776. In one vol., 8vo, old calf, $5.                                    Philadelphia, 1776

SIMS, R. An Index to the Pedigrees and Arms Contained in the Herald's Visitations, and other Genealogical Manuscripts in the British Muesum. 8vo, cloth, pp. 336, $5.          London, 1846

SIMPSON, JAMES H. Journal of a Military Reconnoissance from Santa Fe, New Mexico, to the Navajo Country, made with the Troops under Command of Brevet Lieutenant-Colonel John M. Washington, Chief of the Ninth Military Department, and Governor of New Mexico, in 1849. 8vo, numerous plates, pp. 140, $125.
Philadelphia, 1852

SLATER, SAMUEL, Memoirs of, including a History of the Rise and Progress of Cotton Manufacture in England, and the U. S. 8vo, cloth, $3. 1846

SMITH's History of Virginia, and the Summer Isles, with all the fine old maps. 2 vols., 8vo, boards, uncut, a singularly fine set. Copies in this condition not to be found. $25. Richmond, 1822

SMITH. HORACE W., Nuts for Future Historians to Crack, collected by; containing the Cadwalader Pamphlet, Valley Forge Letters, &c., &c. 8vo, pp. 90, uncut, unbound, $1. Philadelphia, 1856

SMYTH, WILLIAM. Lectures on Modern History, from the Irruption of the Northern Nations, to the Close of the American Revolution. Third American edition Revised and Corrected, with additions, including a preface and a list of books on American History, by Jared Sparks. 8vo, cloth, pp. 760. $1.50. Boston, 1856

SOUTH CAROLINA. Ode to a Friend on our leaving together South Carolina; written in June, 1780. 4to, pp. 15, $2. London, 1783

SOUTH CAROLINA, The Public Laws of the State of, from its First Establishment as a British Province. Down to the Year 1790, Inclusive; in which is Comprehended such of the Statutes of Great Britain as were made of Force by the Act of Assembly of 1712 ; also the Constitution of the United States, and South Carolina, with an Index to the whole. by Hon John F. Grimke. 4to, pp. 682. $10.
Philadelphia, 1790

SOUTH CAROLINA, in the Revolutionary War ; being a Reply to Certain Misrepresentations and Mistakes of Recent Writers in Relation to the Conduct of this State, by a Southron. 12mo. pp. 177. $1.
Charleston, 1853

SPORTING MAGAZINE. The New York, and Annals of the American and English Turf. A work entirely dedicated to sporting subjects and fancy pursuits, occurring in the United States, Canada or Europe, illustrated with engravings, and striking representations of the various subjects, some colored. 4to. vol 1 and 2. $4. New York, 1833—4

SQUIRE. E. G. Antiquities of the State of New York being the Results of Extensive Original Surveys and Explorations, with a Supplement on the Antiquities of the West. Illustrated by fourteen quarto plates and eighty engravings on wood, 8vo, cloth. pp. 334. $1.
Buffalo, 1851

STANBURY. HOWARD. An Expedition to the Valley of the Great Salt Lake of Utah; including a Description of its Geography, Natural History and Minerals, and an Analysis of its Waters ; with an Authentic Account of the Mormon Settlement. Illustrated by numerous plates from drawings taken on the spot. Also a Reconnoissance of a New Route through the Rocky Mountains, and two large and accurate Maps of that region. 2 vols., 8vo, $2.50. Philadelphia, 1855

www.ingramcontent.com/pod-product-compliance
Lightning Source LLC
Chambersburg PA
CBHW021115020726
47500CB00003B/774